Two
IN A
Canoe

GAIL PENDLETON

Print ISBN: 978-1-54393-555-4

eBook ISBN: 978-1-54393-556-1

CHAPTER ONE

The bruise still stung on Becky's cheek, a badge of shame she'd have to bear today.

All night now she had curled up in the back seat of her car, praying that a policeman would not find her here, parked in a lane that meandered down to the Delaware River, a toddler asleep in the car seat in back.

Homeless.

That was what they were now since she stormed out of Mac MacGreavey's house the night before.

He had hit her.

One last hot tear trickled a furrow into the ridges of salt encrusted in the darkening red bruise.

What was she going to do now?

The adrenalin had lasted through packing. Two suitcases were in the trunk. Her quilt covered her. Three grocery bags of food were tucked in beside her. She had really done quite a lot in her fury. And, besides, by now she knew what to grab on the way out the door.

But now what?

She could see the glow of dawn filling up the great bowl of darkness, and knew that today she had to find a place to live. Various child protection services frowned greatly on mothers who did not provide a roof over their children's head. And, if there was one thing Rebecca Rowe was bound and determined to do, it was to stay a step ahead of the child-snatchers. She loved little Daniel with a passion that took her breath away. She was a tigress, fiercely protective of her cub. She would do anything necessary to see that he was safe and fed and loved.

Which one of her friends could she hit on today?

Becky cast her mind over Greenfield, for the hundredth time assessing its possibilities in terms of her need.

The town of Greenfield, where she had grown up, sits beside the Delaware River, its residents engaged in a continual dice game between the elemental river and human attempts at civilization. The flood plain here with its rich, bottomland soil, had attracted an early settler, Cyrus Smith, to its green, unsettled space. He planted a cornfield, grew corn as sweet as cane sugar, and put up a log cabin. On the hills behind the farm, waterfalls dropping off the mountains supplied energy for the mill that ground the corn into meal. Cyrus gave his farm a name -- Greenfield.

The farmer soon discovered that Greenfield, which he had fancied was untamed frontier, was, in fact, at the center of a transportation hub. North and south, the river had a constant traffic of canoes and rafts, and the eastern riverbank was graced by a corduroy road along which wagons rumbled carrying loads of copper ore north to a Hudson dock. East and west – the wilderness trace he had put his feet onto on the way west through the low gaps in the eastern hills – was a well-traveled aboriginal way, feeding out of the Appalachians, a route for the Lenni Lenape and the Iroquois, families hiking together with all their earthly possessions in wicker baskets carried on their backs, to their summer respite at the seashore. The enterprising farmer soon learned that he must accept sea shells among the methods of payment for the ferry that he established at the crossing.

Later settlers found that this track, this path up into the Poconos and into the Appalachians, climbing up the steady slopes behind Greenfield to a mountaintop route where the trees grow stunted and sparse and the days of travel are cool, is a viable route to the riches of the west. Many of the western migrations passed through Greenfield, from the frontier push of the 1750s to the California Gold Rush of the 1850s to the Interstate Highway System of the 1950s. With the river behind them, the western-bound travelers could pause for a rest and a bite to eat in Greenfield before tackling the rise of the mountains west of town. The town became a way station, a final outpost of civilization before the wilderness. Greenfield's merchants were happy to sell to all as they traveled through.

Today, Greenfield creeps up from the riverbank with an arthritic sprawl across floodplain and foothills, never quite sure if Colonial salt-boxes in decay or neoclassical mansions in dry rot set the historical period for the eight-square blocks of civilization poised between river flux and mountain fastness. A bridge, built in the 19th century with stagecoaches in mind, carries Jeep and Chevy and Ford, along with the occasional tractor trailer, from state to state. The Colonial-era inn with its broad, inviting porches is still open in the center of town by the one traffic light, but it looks across at Van Doren's Diner, stainless steel and neon with a spacious parking lot. A 90s-modern supermarket, with winter produce from Mexico and computerized checkout lines, makes town residents very happy, But across the way, Joe's Automotive opens its bay doors on old barn tracks, the real thing still working after a hundred years. Behind the row of stone-solid stores fronting Main Street, the Victorian-style homes fill a few blocks of tree-lined, picture postcard streets. After the Victorian era, the town center was full and building began to stretch out into the foothills, a sprawl of clapboard homes and log cabins with well-appointed kitchens for newfangled housewives and old stone walls preserved for the treasured ambiance. All in all, Greenfield lives on as a tranquil bit of heaven that can't decide if it is part of the 18th century or the 21st.

Reproduction antiques being sold on Main Street are one thing, but cultural mores are another, and it was the cultural mores that had Becky wringing her hands. To Becky, the people of Greenfield seemed living on the edge of cultural schizophrenia, on the one hand watching reruns of Seinfeld with its urban wit, and, on the other, taking a languid slide backward through time to an era of bucolic pseudo wisdom.

Timeless, Becky had heard them call it. The timeless values were promoted at backyard barbecues of rising businessmen, called up at meetings of the school board, and laid out for all to see during social meetings at St. Catherine's Church. There was a right and a wrong in these timeless values, and anybody who wasn't firmly on the side of right was therefore wrong.

For Becky these old-fashioned attitudes had solidified into something unpleasant, something to keep her always on the defensive -- and Becky was tired of being in the wrong.

She wanted a home and a family and a kitchen she could call her own. She wanted those timeless values that she had heard touted. She wanted those common-place things just like any other young woman in Greenfield. She had a baby and all the responsibilities that went along with a family. She just did not have a husband to go with them, and therein was the rub.

Becky was sure that her parents, so up-to-date in so many ways, were straight out of the 18th century in others, Even though they lived in a new home in one of the residential suburbs that stretched back into the valleys, even though her father, a vice-president with Pennsylvania Commonwealth Bank, was a perfectly modern-day executive, their values had come west on that original farm wagon, Becky was sure.

Her "wagon," the one that got her around the town of Greenfield and its environs – uphill, downhill to Wal-Mart and Price Chopper, to Van Doren's Diner and the Dingle Dairy Store, to her friend Barb's apartment and back home again -- was an old blue Dodge four-door sedan. The car had a hundred thousand miles on it, but it still ran with smooth efficiency. Becky babied it. She knew there was none other coming along behind this one – at least not for a long, long time. The car had once sported a soft silvery blue color, entirely suitable for a quiet young woman who liked pretty things, but now the pigments had faded to a slate blue shade, a shadow of the color's former radiance.

The paint was peeling from the front hood, and the rear right fender had a crumpled dent from a long-ago bump in a parking lot. It had come into her life used but eminently functional when she was a senior in high school, a gift from her parents who had only a single child to worry about. She had loved having wheels.

The car was the one thing she had going for her, she knew. Right now, it sat here pulled into the underbrush and holding all her worldly possessions. If some policeman came along to roust her, she'd simply get back in the car and drive back to Mac Macgreavey's house, park in front, and pretend that all was well.

. . . but all was not well.

Becky carefully brushed her curly, red-blonde hair, a heritage from a timeless-values grandmother living in Florida who didn't, so far as Becky knew, have any inkling that she had borne Daniel, that there was a great-grandson out here in the woods waking up for his breakfast, wondering what had happened to his crib.

Single motherhood was not done in her family.

The shock of her pregnancy had sent her mother into hysteria, a real bitch of a fit needing cold compresses and dark, tranquilizers and quiet. Her father talked about shotguns, the old-fashioned way of restoring honor, and lawyers as the prescribed method for today's litigious society.

"Who did this to you?"

Becky thought that was a somewhat strange way of phrasing it since she had been the aggressor in the campfire episode two summers ago. A group of teens, freshly graduated from Greenfield High School, had rented the back field at Carson's Campground for an all-weekend celebration. Robbie Wilson had brought his guitar and sat there by the campfire playing, the firelight flickering warmth across his face, while the group sang the night away. He was such a sexy fox, Becky thought. In the growing glow of dawn light, just like now, Daniel had been created.

Robbie Wilson went on to Brown University that September.

Becky never did answer her father's demanding question, and to her mother's rantings she turned a deaf ear. She started the semester at the county college, dropped out mid-semester, moved in with her friend Karen's parents, who had a spare room, and had Daniel. He was a perfect little boy – auburn hair, brown eyes, the possibility of freckles in the future. For Becky, it was love at first sight. Her parents had not even come to the hospital.

. . . and, oh, yes, there was Public Assistance, which asked the same, damned, demanding question. Becky had no choice this time but to answer – at least she had to answer if she wanted their help -- and so began the blood tests for paternity.

Next thing Becky knew, Robbie Wilson's parents had joined the chorus of voices tugging and pulling at her. Unlike her parents, who preferred to pretend that nothing – even Becky's life – had happened, the Wilsons wanted visitation, wanted something for their money, wanted to make sure their grandson was being cared for. She was still fighting that battle of the Wilsons, but she had answered them the same way she had answered everybody so far.

"I'll do it myself!"

So here she was, Becky mused, as she built a campfire to boil some water for morning coffee and oatmeal. The day-to-day responsibility was all on her shoulders. It would be easier two by two. She knew that now. It didn't take a big brain to figure that one out. -- unless, of course, a woman could earn a big salary that would permit infant care. But Mac MacGreavey, a desperate choice for a provider, had been a bad choice.

Nice little spring here back in the woods. She enjoyed watching the water flow out of the hillside, pooling into a clean, cold, sandy-bottomed, life-sustaining treasure before it bubbled out into a small brook, heading downhill to the river. She knew the spot well, having camped here before. The lane was used by fishermen heading for the river just beyond, but nobody had ever disturbed her here at the spring. She filled her coffee pot with water and hooked it to the tripod set up over the fire.

Aarggh. If only I could turn myself into two people, she mused -- one to work and the other to take care of Daniel. Or into a teacher or lawyer who makes the money to have a nanny, like something you see on TV. That would be nice. That was the idea of motherhood she'd had before the reality had descended upon her. Now the concept of a professional life was far beyond her comprehension; she struggled just to keep the day-to-day needs taken care of.

She pulled the coffee pot off the hook, added half a cup of boiling water to Daniel's oatmeal and half a cup to hers, filled the coffee cup, and added a spoonful of instant coffee and a spoonful of sugar.

Potty training -- that was the answer. As soon as Daniel was potty-trained, day care would become more affordable, and she could get a job. Boys are slower, she had been warned; don't even try before he was two, her friends had suggested. Come next summer, though, she was going to have to work on this effort.

Sipping her coffee, she watched the silver mist rising, drifting through the liquid-gold woods. Sunlight dropped shifting patterns through the thinning trees. A squirrel family chittered to her left, getting ready for another day of collecting acorns. It wasn't supposed to be so hard raising a child. A tear dropped down Becky's cheek, unbidden. She wiped it away with the back of her hand.

Daniel, waking up in his car seat, started to fuss. Becky ran to the car, comforting him.

"Shh, shh, Little boy. It's okay. Mommy's here."

She fumbled with the buckles of the car seat, unlatching them finally, and then lifted him out of the close space.

He arched his back and kicked his legs as she laid him down on the back seat to change his diaper.

"Ready for a stretch, heh?"

The space was tight, and Becky took a kick to the arm. She'd have another bruise in that spot, but she tried hard not to hurt. A little mind power would take care of it. Such was the price of parenthood, after all.

Daniel smiled a good morning smile at Becky, his teeth in a majestic white arc against the pink of his lips, and she melted.

After his breakfast, Becky let him run for a bit. She liked to watch her son play like this. She could see the man in the boy, just as she had seen the boy in the infant they had first handed her. Becky liked being a mother. She thought she was a natural mother. She felt entirely competent to deal with the growing person, the independent person, who was her son. If only it weren't for the continual problem of the roof over their heads.

"Come on. Race ya!"

He giggled, and the two of them ran up the lane, arms and legs flapping, leaves crunching underfoot. "Cocka doodle do!" They both laughed. Good way to start the morning, Becky mused, her eyes twinkling now.

She squared her shoulders to hold the twinkle steady as she re-packed the car and headed for town to find a bed for tonight.

Behind her, the river winked in the sunlight and rolled on, a watery slash through September's brown-and-gold tweed landscape.

CHAPTER TWO

"Hey, I've got a place you can stay for a while."

The voice was not a familiar one, so Becky turned her head warily. Offers of a place to live just did not come out of the blue.

"Do I know you?" She raised an eyebrow quizzically.

"I'm Lou. Lou Maltafozza." From the other end of the lunch counter, a middle-aged man, paunchy and balding, raised a frosty glass in greeting.

"Do you know this guy, Barb?" Becky asked the waitress. Barb had just turned her down. No room in her tiny apartment, she had said. Besides, she had a grouchy landlord who had an aversion to little children. As much as she loved Becky and Daniel, it just wouldn't work.

"Sure! Lou! He comes in here all the time." Barb gave another wipe to the counter in front of her, trailing water from an orange- and yellow-check dish rag.

"Is he okay?" Becky asked as she stared back at Lou, sizing him up, assessing what she would have to do for this roof over her head.

"Sure. Far as I know, he's not an axe murderer."

"Umm."

Lou stared back, tilting his head to the right and then the left. Was he assessing her? What nerve!

"The customers seated between them stared back and forth, hamburgers forgotten, their heads swiveling at the unexpected drama.

"Old Lou's getting a girlfriend." Somebody tittered.

"No. It's not like that at all," Lou said. "I've got this place that I'm closing up for the season. Could really use a caretaker there, somebody to clean the place up a bit and make it look lived in. The girl needs a place to live. She can use the place long as it doesn't cost me any money."

A smile spread across Becky's face, sunshine breaking through a crack in the black fog of her current dilemma.

"Really?"

"Really!"

His answering grin was impish, a look totally unrelated to the reality as Becky understood it. She thought they were making a business arrangement, but that interior warning bell started going ding, ding, ding. She raised her eyebrows.

"You have something up your sleeve."

Caution was the better part of valor. Becky knew all the aphorisms, as well as all the stories. She'd done a lot of reading as a kid.

"No. No sleeves! See!" Lou held up two hairy arms, bare to above the elbows. "Caretaker. I need a caretaker. That's all. Wanna do some raking and such to earn your rent? No salary – just a place to stay. I don't want the place to become a hangout or broken into. I need the lights on, television blaring, smoke coming from the chimney, leaves raked out of the parking lot -- just ordinary living issues. You can do that for me?"

His voice rose to a question mark.

"Sure."

"Barb, get this girl a hamburger on me. Yeh, feed the kid, too. I'll go next door to the hardware store and get this key copied."

He held out his right hand for a shake, and Becky, adjusting Daniel on her hip, took it. He pumped with a firm, two-handed grip. A deal had been struck.

A place to stay, a roof over their heads! Becky blinked in amazement.

A sign at the turnoff announced the Duck Point Inn. A cutout wooden fish caught in on arched jump formed the backdrop for rustic log letters. The D was peeling, and letters had fallen away. Becky could see the outline of less-faded paint where the word "Inn" had once been.

Becky turned the wheel, her old sedan following Lou's white Cadillac into the dark woods, gravel crunching underneath the tires. The one lane led downward, through an evergreen forest, and then switch-backed through tangled rhododendron and misshapen trees to a lower level at river's edge. She could feel her car suspension groaning as it contracted where the road was banked or hit bottom on the washouts.

Becky caught her breath against a slash of fear. What are you doing, girl? What are you doing really? Going down into the woods with a man you don't know!

If there had been a place to turn around, she would have angled her car and fled for the safety of sunlight above. But in this narrowness there was only one direction – down.

Breaking through the trees, finally, into a small clearing at the bottom of the gorge, she could see the inn.

The building leaned in full fishing-camp, ramshackle regalia along the riverbank, siding canted every which way, a crazy quilt of logs and shingles and roofing and bricks, with a long gray porch agape beneath the glittering eyes of windows, steps to the river stretching a scarecrow arm into the gold and lavender brush of weeds at the river's edge.

"You're the answer to my prayers, Sweetheart," Lou said. "I need somebody to keep an eye on this place, actually. Kids break in sometimes, do vandalism. It would be nice if the place looked like it was lived in."

"What is this place?"

"A fishing camp: restaurant, boat access, rooms for rent upstairs. Closed for the season early this year. My partner had a heart attack, and I can't run it alone. So? You willing to keep an eye on this place for me?"

"Sure." She danced a little dance of eagerness on the gravel parking lot, treading down her fear, raising up the rewards – a real place to live, not trying to fit into somebody's life, not the third wheel, not the scullery maid nor the bed partner.

Looking to Daniel, she saw that he was asleep in the car seat in the back of the sedan. She decided to let him finish his nap. He was safe here. Quietly, she opened the car window so he'd have some air while she explored.

Lou handed her a key. She turned it in the lock and entered.

She was enchanted. The first thing she saw was the chandelier, a wooden and brass wagon wheel sporting electric candles, hung from a high ceiling with brass chains. Then, she saw the dark beams soaring into this cavernous space, the knotty pine covering the walls, the knobs and curls and cutouts of wooden gingerbread arching in the corners. Next, a stone fireplace, floor to ceiling of field stones, caught her eye. Finally, her senses drew in the lace curtains, the velvet cushions on the carved chairs, the silver flower vases on each table.

"This is like something out of a fairy tale," she gasped.

"More like a nightmare to me," Lou replied.

But how did it come to be? This is fabulous." She spread her arms wide taking in the rustic luxury of the large public dining room.

"Actually, it was designed after the hunting lodges of Bavaria and Austria." Lou grinned, a smirk of pride at the edges of his smile as he recounted the story. "Kings and counts all had their hunting lodges. They were quite the rage in the nineteenth century. This building dates from the nineteenth century, too, believe it or not."

"Oh, I believe it."

Lou went on. "It was built to draw rich sportsmen to the fishing here. Take a look at the photos on the walls."

He whipped a handkerchief out of his back pocket and wiped the grime off a couple of the framed sepia-toned photos.

She peered closer.

"That one is Babe Ruth. Here is Teddy Roosevelt."

Becky recognized the figure, familiar from her history textbooks, standing in a pair of tan rubber waders in the middle of a brook, fishing pole arched in front, ready for business. In another ornately framed photo, Babe Ruth had a string of fat fish and a satisfied smile on his round pride-of-the-Yankees face.

"The nice thing about this location. . . ? The Mongaup joins the river just upstream. It's got the best trout fishing on the whole East Coast, maybe the best in the world, and, in front of the lodge is the river itself, with its bass and shad. So a fisherman can have his choice – and a full season of fishing from spring through fall."

It was not hard to believe Lou's patter; something had obviously happened here once, but where were all these fabled fishermen today? The inn echoed as the footsteps of Lou and Becky broke the silence.

Becky looked around her at the dust and grime that competed with the rustic luxury for attention. She realized the velvet was faded, the silver tarnished, the wooden decorations covered with cobwebs and dust. She wrinkled her nose in distaste.

"How come you closed?"

"Like I said, I can't run this place all by myself."

"Woodstove." He took her into the inn's bar, tucked underneath a balcony in a separate room. "That's better heat than the fireplace. Wood pile's out back, far end of the parking lot, but if you plan to stay for the winter, you'd better cut more. You can have your choice of bedrooms. Sheets need washing, though. There's the kitchen, back there -- could stand a little cleaning up."

Sure could, Becky thought as she entered through the swinging doors. The kitchen was a pigpen, with trash piled up everywhere. Cans bulged with black bags waiting for disposal; lids tilted over the fullness, and a mouse skittered away as they approached. The floor was black with grease layered in the corners where the mop had not reached. The wall behind the stove was streaked with gravy and coffee stains. Even the ceiling was yellow with a layer of grime and cobweb.

She ran her finger across the top white stoneware plate in a cupboard, and the finger came away sticky. She added two eyes to the design on the plate, making a smiley face in the coating. A lot of cooking went on here, she realized, but apparently over the years nobody knew how to clean. Her mouth mirrored the resigned smile she had given the plate.

Their footsteps echoed on the grubby black-and-tan-check tile floor as she followed Lou into still another room beyond, a store, with all the gear and accessories needed by an old-time fisherman. This stock was all lying unsold, though, gently transforming into antique status with each passing day. Fishing rods and reels, an assortment of flies, hip boots, hats, baskets, nets, and, behind the register, two dozen crampons waited in an unwanted neglect, cobwebs and fly specks everywhere. Faded tee shirts emblazoned with the Duck Point Inn logo spoke of a previous life, now forgotten.

With her finger she drew a squiggle in the dust on the counter, fighting against the sense of abandonment she felt.

"Eat up those snacks if you want. They won't be any good by spring."

Lou pointed to several cartons, unopened under the counter. The cartons lacked the coating of grunge that predominated in this room. They looked new.

Becky looked closely. She realized they were this year's supply of snacks. Something here, for once, was current.

Becky nodded her head, assenting to the devouring of Devil Dogs and Doritos, Baby Ruths and Chee-tos.

She sighed. She really did not want to clean up this greasy kitchen, to rake out the parking lot, to cut wood for the stove, but it was the middle of September, and the nights were getting damn cold for sleeping in the car.

They exchanged phone numbers. Becky wrote Lou's number in a small notebook she kept in her purse. He had an official-looking, faux-leather datebook that he opened with a flourish and snapped shut after recording her name and cell-phone number.

Together they walked back to the cars. Becky waved goodbye as Lou's Cadillac, crunching on gravel, headed up the drive, climbed the bank, went through the trees, and was gone. She was alone. She tucked the key into her purse.

"Well, Daniel, here we are. Our very own fishing camp -- just what I always wanted." She giggled as she leaned in to release him from the belt, waking him up. "Let's go make ourselves at home."

. . . and home it very quickly became.

Becky picked the first bedroom from the stairs. One window faced south, giving sunlight for most of the day, while another had a view of the river. A floor grate was open to the bar below, where the wood stove crackled through the evening, and the heat flowed upward. The room had a mahogany four-poster bed with a cotton eyelet dust ruffle and a quilted coverlet, for which a thorough washing did wonders.

She plugged her small television into an outlet in the bar and, to her delight, the cable worked. A small sink and two-burner portable stove were available, so she set up her kitchen and living room here. It felt cozier than the large, open dining room and cleaner than the grease-coated kitchen. Once she had her own microwave plugged in and her own dishes on the shelf, she felt right at home. She moved the bar stock to an upper cupboard where Daniel could not reach it.

Then, she set about cleaning and clearing throughout the inn. She raked, and she scrubbed, and she chopped wood. The showers did not work – none of them gave forth even a dribble -- but one claw-foot bath tub had fittings that worked. She scoured the tub, boiled water in a large teapot, and did her best to make a bath with that. At night she luxuriated in the inch of hot water before falling between the sheets in the romantic, double bed in the bedroom above.

This wasn't going to last, she realized, staring at the knot-holed ceiling, the warm pattern of log rafters giving comforting shelter as the rain pounded on the roof. For one thing, the end of October meant the water would have to be turned off, the pipes drained. How were water pipes to survive in a house without central heating? Becky wondered if Lou would come back to drain the pipes, or did he expect her as caretaker to do that job? Then she asked herself, How would she get by here in the winter without running water?

Was the answer in that shed that really was an outhouse disguised as a shed? Could she make it through the winter if she chopped enough wood?

But would that stove really keep the place warm?

And how would she get out of here once the weather deposited ice and snow on the steep lane to the highway?

Happy though she was, she couldn't stop the anxiety from rising in her chest and clogging her throat with fear that, somehow, this would not work out and she'd be back in the car again, knocking on doors, looking for a place to live for herself and Daniel.

CHAPTER THREE

In the early days of October, Becky found some time to sit on the porch of the Duck Point Inn relaxing in the warm afternoons and getting acquainted with this new environment.

She soon came to know that one of the constant sounds echoing throughout the valley, surprisingly enough, was the roar of motorcycles. A road snaked along about two-thirds of the way up the cliff face opposite the Duck Point Inn. The cars that traveled the road caused only a gentle hum of traffic noise to come to the inn, a hum almost not noticed by a modern-day human used to the constant sound vibration of the 21st century world. During the daytime, the car sounds came and went overhead like the wind swishing through the trees. At night, Becky often saw the flash of headlights as a car rounded the curves, and she heard the vehicle but simply added its descant to the harmony of nature that lulled her to sleep. Motorcycles, however, were quite another matter.

Va, Va, Voom. Bzzzz.

Voom, bang, va, voom, bzzzz.

Zzzzzz! (shift) Zzzzzzzz! (shift) Zzzzzzzzzzz!

Zzsshzzsshzzsshzzsshzzsshzz. Va voom! Boom!

Within a matter of days living at the inn, Becky had come to distinguish the Harleys from all the other variety of motorcycle. They emitted a deep-throated roar that echoed off the cliff face and filled the valley with sound. Harleys were the testosterone of the motorcycle world, Becky understood. They were the biggest, the baddest, the best. At least, they sounded the loudest in the fantasy Becky was weaving on those solitary days of early October. She'd never paid much attention to motorcycles before. Occasionally, on a summer day on the road, she'd pass a platoon of bikers, handlebars and knees at attention as the group of ten, or thirty, or fifty bikers rode past her. These interactions usually happened on a Sunday afternoon when all of the New York metropolitan area – along with the Connecticut and New Jersey suburbs -- spilled over into the narrow and winding back roads of the Poconos to enjoy the mountain scenery.

She remembered once when, seeing such a group, she had inquired of her father, "Is that a motorcycle gang?"

He had replied back, "No. Not really. I'd call it a motorcycle club."

She'd been about eight then, a kid who still was more interested in her dolls than the open road. Apparently she'd paid enough attention through the years, though, to recognize the sound of a Harley, a sound that moved now from the back to the forefront of her brain.

What are these bikers doing? she wondered.

They'd go back and forth, back and forth, turning around at each end of the cliff road and going through the curves again, each pass louder than the one before. Finally, it dawned on her they were doing heats. They were riding in front of the cliff face listening to the sound of their full-throttled engines, the louder the better, echo back at them. The Harleys definitely had it over all the others, with their subterranean bass, but even the more treble bikes sounded impressive as their exuberant roar bounced back and forth and filled the gorge.

Ha! In a flash, she understood the biker's passion, their game. She came to appreciate the endurance it took to go back and forth, back and forth, back and forth, making your mark on the world. . . I mean, why have a loud engine if you can't have a little fun with it?

A musician could make much of this, she mused -- *The Biker Symphony*. She laughed at her own joke.

She thought about her own life. Maybe she should make a bit more noise, run heats along the cliff face and do some therapeutic yelling. This noise sounded positively liberating. She'd have to do it with Daniel in tow, though. That wouldn't have quite the same free-ing effect. Still, that rumble of noise reverberating through the valley every so often came for Becky to represent a working out of her own frustrations, a long primal scream of the id, a making of her own dis-tinctive mark on the world; she smiled whenever she heard it. She cheered them on, and she cheered herself on. Go, girl. Go!

CHAPTER FOUR

Becky's wait at the Public Assistance Office seemed endless. She had gotten a letter to come in and see her caseworker. Her anxiety bubbled hotly in her throat. What was wrong now? To make the wait even harder, Daniel would not sit still. He squirmed out of her lap, escaping her restraining arms.

"Car."

Daniel ran up the hallway toward the exit door, sneakers pattering on the tiled floor.

Becky moved into his view, hands on hips, face showing displeasure. When, he didn't respond, she followed him down the hallway, picked him up, and carried him back to the waiting room.

"Sit here."

"Do you want to eat something? Pretzels? Or fishy crackers? Or Bologna?"

Becky unfolded the cellophane package and showed it to him.

He jabbed a chubby finger at the picture on the package.

"Yes, those are the planets – Saturn and Venus."

She knew he wouldn't remember the names, but she wanted to get into the habit of telling him things, teaching him.

"Look, here's a toy."

He took the small plastic figure.

"Is it working? Let me see."

"Hey, Mommy."

He slid off the chair, blue sweat pants brushing against the cracked plastic seat, and headed up the hallway again, his sneakers pattering in a high-spirited rhythm.

"Come here. Back"

This time, she didn't try to coax him to return. With three big strides, she had him under the arms. She picked him up and settled him back in the chair.

"Ab dab do."

"Stay here."

Finally, it was her turn. Hearing her name, she slung the diaper bag and her purse on one shoulder, and picked Daniel up in her arms. She followed her caseworker down an interior hallway to an office, small and piled high with folders and boxes. Late afternoon sun shone wanly through one dirty window, reflecting off dust motes floating lazily above the clutter.

Becky picked her way through the aisle cleared in the middle of all this. She settled herself into the hard-backed chair that was offered and sat Daniel on her lap.

"How are you today?" The caseworker's smile seemed searching. Becky wondered if she'd done something wrong -- missed a form, perhaps, or didn't bring in required proofs in time.

"I've been trying to call you."

"My cell phone is cranky."

"Oh?" The caseworker's eyebrows rose above her glasses frame; her forehead pushed up in concentric ridges. Becky wondered if that arched look of surprise was the origin of the question mark.

"I really don't know what is wrong with it, and I don't have the money to buy another."

"I see. Well, that is why I wrote you a letter. You do still have that post office box?"

"Yes."

"Umph. Good."

The caseworker paused for a moment, taking a deep breath of the stale air. Without exhaling, she asked, "Where are you living these days?"

. . . the dreaded question. Becky squirmed on the hard wooden chair. Daniel was a dead weight in her lap.

"The Duck Point Inn," she mumbled. Her mouth felt dry, the words cottony.

"Where's that?"

"Up the river road about 15, 20 miles, down by the river."

". . . still in this county?"

"Yes."

"Are you paying rent there?"

"No, I am working for my room."

The caseworker's mouth turned downward. She focused abruptly. "Are you getting a salary?"

"No. No salary."

"Be careful you don't change your eligibility."

"I will." The perspiration popped out on Becky's forehead. "I'd really like to get my own place. Could you find some money for that somewhere? How am I doing on the Section 8 waiting list? "

"You're still on the list, but nobody has moved off." The case-worker raised her hands in a teepee and tapped her fingers. ". . . could take years actually."

The caseworker looked thoughtful for a moment.

"We could give you five hundred a month toward rent if you decide to get your own place."

"Where am I going to find an apartment for five hundred a month?"

"True, true."

A silence hung heavily in the office. Becky felt claustrophobic.

"Sometimes two moms will get together and rent a small house." The caseworker's voice drifted off. "Of course, you have to know somebody you will get along with."

"Right!"

Then, the woman's mood changed.

". . . and, oh, here. This is why I called you in. We had some donations."

The caseworker rummaged in a corner; the back of her plaid, polyester skirt was momentarily Becky's entire field of view in the small office. She came up with a huge, white shopping bag, and, smiling, she brought forth a dark blue quilted jacket with hood and matching blue quilted snow pants, just Daniel's size.

"It's going to be getting cold soon. You can have this for Daniel."

"Oh, thank you."

". . . and here." She kept rummaging in the bag. Out came another quilted polyester coat, this time a prettier, more feminine blue with a sporty stripe on the sleeve – quite attractive, as a matter of fact.

"Do you need a coat, too? This one should fit you."

"Thank you," Becky said with the tone of her voice upturned into a smile. It really was a very nice winter jacket. She was pleased.

On Becky's way back to the inn, the breeze was brisk, blowing leaves across the road in whirlwinds of red and orange debris. Well, every little bit helps, Becky reflected. Now, I will not have to spend the money to buy warm coats for us.

She did have to buy diapers and dish soap, shampoo and sanitary napkins, socks and sneakers, sweat shirts and sweaters, hats and mittens. The seasons were changing, and she had to prepare for colder weather for both of them. At Wal-Mart she shopped carefully, according to her list. The jeans she bought for Daniel were a bit too loose and long; she could always fold up the cuffs for a while as he grew into them. He was growing like a weed, so they'd fit soon enough.

Later, Becky counted out her money. She folded a $20 bill over and tucked it into the inside zipper pocket of her purse. She smiled. Her little stash was up to $200 now. She was saving for a month-and-a-half security plus the first month's rent. She had a long way to go.

CHAPTER FIVE

The river starts with an uprush of water escaping the mountain stronghold of Precambrian granite. Here, on this wild slope, in the ice caverns and prehistoric lairs, live the gods of thunder, the trolls and gnomes of legend, the wild beasts of the id wreaking their destructions upon the crags and gullies of the wilderness.

The water gurgles up into a spring, shot through with sifted, silver sand, and then soaks through a mat of watercress into a creek where it tumbles joyfully over the gravel and rocks, seeking its downhill destiny It is an uneven going, like a toddler trying out its first steps, but, like a toddler growing into a child, once set free, the water is relentless on its quest for the sea.

The creek meanders through a wild-flower meadow, lush with minnows and amoeba, makes an exhilarating adolescent rush down a rocky slope, catches its breath as it leaps off a cliff, splashes around a boulder, leaps again. The mist shimmers into a rainbow, one end touching the watery pool, the other reaching skyward in a colorful highway to heaven. Playful, prayerful, the river goes, trying out its muscle as it grows with every added drop.

Lower down the mountain, the water plays with trout, dancing in through the gills, caressing the scales, rushing with growing force around hip waders of fishermen. It tickles the webbed feet of frogs, and slithers off the feathers of wading birds come to feed.

Then, grasping hands with other rivulets that come leaping off the mountainside, the creek suddenly becomes the river, a muted roar of power that spreads its maturity in the wide bed it still carves for itself from the rock of creation. Whitewater marks the upper reaches of the river, where rocks form impediments and shelves, and the shallow water teases the hulls of canoes.

Later, the river settles in for its run to the sea, a sunshine-reflecting surface split by the vees of ducks and shad, outboards stirring up algae and wakes. Finally, closer to the bay, the water dons a royal necklace of bridges and lights and rumbles its sea-going majesty through a festive panorama of cities and commerce and civilization.

Through it all, the river rolls on, smug in its forces of heaven and hell. Here, in the river's watery environs, is the constructive beat of life itself, which could not exist without the water's ancient alchemy. Yet, here, in the water's power, also is the most destructive force on Earth.

Given enough time, could a river split the planet in two?

Becky woke with a start. A door had closed. She listened carefully in the dawn silence. A toilet flushed. A downstairs toilet. The one that opened onto the river-front porch.

Her throat constricted with fear. She wanted nothing more than to pull the quilt over her head and pretend she'd heard nothing, but she knew she could not. She was alone here with Daniel, and whatever happened was up to her to deal with.

Gingerly, she got out of bed and tiptoed over to the door. She could hear the clump, clump of hiking boots on the porch. She pushed open the window a crack and peered out. No one was in sight, but a green-and-yellow canoe was pulled up on the riverbank.

Aha. It was a would-be customer. That answered some of the questions. Becky took a deep breath, and then another, pushed her shoulders back and went marching out to send him on his way.

Closed. She needed a closed sign on the riverside bank, too, as well as up at the road, where she had already nailed the definitive word. Of course a canoeist would want to stop here! He was expecting breakfast probably! She tap, tapped down the outside stairway.

Suddenly she heard a crash and the sound of a body falling. Curses rippled up from the porch.

She raced to the porch and scrambled to the steps, which no longer were all in one piece.

The first thing she saw was the gun.

Holstered and strapped to his hip, it still gave her pause. Then, she saw that the pistol was backed by a uniform -- khaki with a green, embroidered shoulder patch – a national park ranger.

He was sprawled on the ground below the broken steps, a cluster of wooden shards on the ground beside him.

"Are you hurt? What happened?"

"The porch step broke underneath me." He grimaced in pain and waved a piece of board at her. "Look! It was rotten."

"Yes, there's a lot of this place like that I've noticed."

He winced as he tried to get up,

"Here! Let me help you. Do you think you need an ambulance?"

"No. I just twisted it. Let me sit for a moment."

He leaned back against the porch railing and gave Becky a quizzical look.

She realized she was standing there in flannel pajamas and fuzzy slippers. Her hair was probably standing upright in the back where she'd lain on the pillow.

"So who are you? I didn't expect anybody to be here."

"I might ask the same question of you. Who are you, and what are you doing here?" Becky tried to look stern. She felt, though, as if the questions were coming from far, far away.

"I'm Parker Sims, and I'm the ranger in charge of this stretch of the river. Lou and Nate always let me make a pit stop here when I'm on patrol."

"Oh, I see. Well, we're closed." Becky had had the words on her mouth for five minutes, just waiting to drop them and get it over with. "We're closed." She tilted her head, birdlike, and looked at him.

My! He was a good-looking man. The realization struck her with surprise. He had dirty blonde hair that fell over his tanned forehead, a la Indiana Jones. Green eyes twinkled. And were those laugh lines beside his eyes?

Suddenly, she felt shy.

"Closed?"

"Yes. I'm the caretaker."

"What happened to Lou and Nate?"

"Lou brought me down here. He said his partner had a heart attack."

Parker Sims' laugh lines eased out into an expression of concern. "Oh, darn. I hope he's okay."

Becky suddenly felt guilty at never grieving for the mysterious Nate, the blank piece of this Duck Point Inn puzzle.

It was as if he read her thoughts. "Don't fret over it. I'll call Lou."

"Is my face that much of an open book?"

In response, she could feel his eyes traveling over her face, tracing the contours of her cheeks, brushing against her eyelashes, touching her chin with a caress. She blushed, the hot burn working its way up from her bosom to her neck to her cheeks.

"I say," he commented with an uncharacteristic gravity. "I think I should come back without the uniform."

There was a long silence as the suggestion hung between them, his eyes on her face, her face filled with fire.

"May I?" His tone was gentle. "I mean, I don't want to harass you. I'm on duty and all that, so I'll just go away if you want, but I'd really like to get to know you better – if that's okay with you."

"Yes," she stammered. "Of course. I should tell you though. There is Daniel."

Disappointment brushed across his face, and he tilted his head questioningly at her. His mouth twisted in dismay.

"Husband? Boyfriend?"

"No. My son."

A grin split his sorrow asunder. "Yee haw!"

The shout echoed from the walls, shot across the water, and came back to them from the cliffs on the other bank.

She smiled. His joy was transparent.

"Shh!" She put a finger to her mouth, grinning impishly. "You'll wake him"

"Good. I want to meet him." His smile stretched even more broadly. Laugh lines crinkled in the tanned cheeks, and Becky could see even white teeth – a perfect smile if ever there was one.

She put her hand to her mouth, unsure of the appropriateness of the chortle that was erupting. Then, she gave in to a joyous laugh, a sound she thought she had forgotten to make. Suddenly, all was right with the world.

That evening he came back, bringing a huge steak, Italian bread, salad makings. They worked side by side cutting and chopping, side by side grilling.

Parker and Daniel wrestled a bit on the grass, both man and boy giggling.

"Do you know how to play baseball, yet?" Parker asked him, "Do you know how to paddle a canoe?"

"No," Daniel announced loudly. "Cookie."

"No cookie. Milk."

"No muk!"

"What? No milk?" Parker pretended shock. "How are you going to grow into a baseball player?"

"Oh, he's just got that word 'no' down pat," Becky said, laughing.

She handed Daniel a sippy cup, and he sat down on the grass before putting the spout into his mouth. Milk dribbled down his chin, and Becky wiped it with a paper towel.

He'll never go to sleep with all this excitement, she thought..

At Daniel's bedtime, they worked side by side putting him to bed. He did take the bed-time bottle, holding it firmly with his right hand while he sucked, and he clutched his Thomas the Tank Engine blanket with his left hand, rubbing it against his face for comfort. His features coalesced into the contentment of warmth and full belly, and soon his whole body relaxed into sleep. Becky took the bottle away from him, and she and Parker tiptoed out of the room, turning off the light as they went.

Later, sitting downstairs, Parker asked Becky, "Do you know how to paddle a canoe?"

"Can't say I do."

"We still have time for a lesson or two before the weather turns."

They were washing the grill – side by side – in the deep sink in the main kitchen. Parker doused the grill in the hot soapy water, scouring with a Brillo pad.

"For it's hi ho, and off to work we go." Parker sent a rousing baritone chorus into the cavernous kitchen, rattling the dark, cobwebbed corners with vibrations.

"What do you think this is? The home of the Seven Dwarfs?" Becky laughed as she dried.

"Sure. Look at this place."

"I'm glad somebody besides me sees the resemblance."

"I do. I do. I knew them well, but even more important – I learned a lesson from those little dwarfs who used to live here."

"What lesson is that?"

"Always keep singing. Keep singing. Lessens the pain."

She raised an eyebrow at him.

" 'With a yo ho, Blow the man down.' I'm not staying the night you know."

"Nobody asked you to stay the night."

" 'Rub a dub dub, Two men in a tub.' Just taking that weight off your back."

Her mouth pursed into a huge "oh".

"Of course, that doesn't say I won't ever stay the night -- later on – if you'll have me of course."

"This is an inn. There are plenty of bedrooms."

She worked hard to keep a straight face. Then, she giggled. He winked at her. She smiled back. She slathered a creamy white lotion on her hands and offered the bottle to him. He accepted it without a word, just a play of smiles and ripples and interesting angles across his expressive face.

Two by two, she pondered. If this were the dwarfs' cottage and she were Snow White, could this be Prince Charming? But then she remembered; that story also had a witch in disguise – and she did not want a witch in any form. Don't get so excited, she told herself. He's not a prince, and he's not the villain of the piece, either. He's merely saying, let's go slow here. Let's not rush into anything. And she couldn't fault that -- not one bit – even though her feet had danced with excitement when she heard his four-wheel-drive pickup truck crunching on the gravel of the drive.

Time passed, a crescendo of color rising to brighten their lives as September flowed over into October, and they began to know one another.

CHAPTER SIX

The river flowed through a liquid gold tunnel now, water surface reflecting the color of the riverbanks. The whole world felt to Becky like the inside of a Butterfinger candy bar, gold and striated and dropping off sugary flakes of melt-in-your mouth goodness with every touch.

Every weekend the canoeists and rafters were out there on the river. All afternoon, every time Becky paused to look out a window, there was a canoe or a raft somewhere in view – sometimes a bevy of them.

"Summertime is wall-to-wall canoes and rafts. It's a non-stop party on the river," Parker had told her, "But now is when you can see the river when you go canoeing."

So Becky donned an orange life preserver, taking up a paddle herself.

Parker had brought two friends, Dave and Pamela, for a weekday outing, since he was on duty and patrolling the river weekends when the crowds were out and about, but Mondays and Tuesdays were his.

As it turned out, they now were hers, too, in this new reality that pleased her immensely.

In order to go out canoeing on the river, though, she would have to leave Daniel with Dave and Pamela, who also would prepare the barbecue for their return. The scenario had been prearranged by Parker.

"I'm not sure he'll stay with them. He'll scream," Becky protested.

"Pam's a pre-school teacher. She can handle him."

Sure enough! Pamela arrived with a dump truck, digging tools, and a huge bag of sand. She looked prepared for an army of 18-month-olds.

Going down the rickety wooden stairs, Becky heard Daniel's wails at being abandoned and felt her own guilt at abandoning him. She rarely left him. The child's clinging, growing body had become attached to her, almost a growth on her hip where he sat astraddle, and certainly a growth on her brain where it curled around his constant presence, his constant needs. Now, for a brief time, that part of her would be chopped away and left behind.

"Don't you ever leave him with a babysitter?" asked Pamela.

"No," admitted Becky sheepishly.

But Parker's expectation coerced. He wanted a day alone on the water with her.

Besides, the adventure beckoned. She really did want to get into that canoe and go floating down the river of gold, merging into a transcendental oneness with the beauty of water and land and sky. She forced herself to focus on the task at hand, getting ready for the river trip.

The canoe was heavier than she had thought. She gathered her strength and heaved the canoe until it slid off the rocks, floating free in the gentle backwash near the river bank.

She adjusted the unfamiliar life preserver, planted her feet carefully on a slippery rock and assessed the situation. Somehow she had to get into that canoe, bobbing back and forth now with a mind of its own.

"There now, don't be afraid to get your feet wet," Parker shouted. "Step in the water."

She looked at him. It seemed so effortless. He stepped in, the canoe shifted to accommodate his weight, and he slid down onto his seat.

"Now, you. Remember the canoe has to be balanced. We work together."

She hung onto the two sides of the canoe and stepped in, feeling the canoe jounce hard underneath her.

"Careful."

Sitting down onto her seat waiting for the next stage, she realized that her feet where they were wet were freezing. The river, unlike the ocean, which retains its heat well into October, cools down quickly in the fall. Each chill night had leached a little more warmth from the waters tumbling down the mountainsides in their incessant journey.

Parker, on the rear seat, pushed against the rocks with his paddle, and the canoe floated free. She felt the craft bounce underneath her as it found its buoyancy in the watery element, and suddenly she and the canoe were weightless, adrift in the liquid gold, caught by the current, heading downstream.

She gasped with the unexpected pleasure of the passage.

Then, she tried to remember her shore lessons. Hold the paddle just so. Dip. Push. Lift.

"Remember, I'm doing most of the work back here," said Parker's disembodied voice behind her. She was afraid to turn and look for fear of upsetting the balance. "I want you to get the feel of the paddle and what it will do in the water."

She nodded. She paddled. The canoe headed downstream, and she realized that a lot of the effort of this was merely keeping the canoe heading in the right direction, going with the flow. Her arms began to ache, and she gritted her teeth. Four miles to go. She grimaced. She had not anticipated the endurance needed. She had not expected the pain.

"Oh, look. Look at that!"

A blue heron, gray silhouette against the hazy gold, picked its stately way through the rocks and weeds at water's edge, each leg lifted at a sharp angle as it moved. Ducks paddling in a string worked their way upstream, adolescents in an eager line behind mom and dad.

Bank weeds cut a muted purple slash through the gold. Becky laid the paddle across the wales of the canoe, resting for a moment and marveling at the beauty that surrounded her. In the silence, she could hear the ripples and the splashes, the jumps around her, even the sound of clouds passing overhead – or was that the wind? Whatever it was, she held her face up to it gratefully, happy to be a part of this nature.

"Do you like?" Parker's voice floated behind her.

"Oh, yes."

"Is this the first time you've been in a canoe?"

"Yes."

"I thought so."

"Being transparent again, was I?"

"You aren't looking at the river, enjoying it. You are focused on the sitting and the paddling."

"You're right. I had no idea what a canoe was like."

"Didn't you go to camp when you were a kid?"

Becky felt no judgment with the question; his voice was open with simple curiosity. She felt the warmth as he waited for her response.

"I went to arts and crafts camp. I also spent a lot of time in the library."

Dip, splash. The paddle hit the water.

"I see."

"Relax! Enjoy it."

He was right; she hadn't been looking at the river. In fact, she hadn't been looking around at the world outside herself at all.

Nesting! That is what she had been doing, Nesting, like those ducks, who during the spring season had had the bowl-like clump of grass hidden somewhere where the ducklings were hatched, keeping a wary eye out for foxes. She had watched their antics enough times on television's Discovery Channel to know the nesting routine.

She watched the ducks, which were now and then diving under the water searching for a fingerling or picnic crumb. The canoe was close enough to them that she could see them change from gently bobbing cork into sleek, purposeful hunting machine under the water. They didn't worry about where their next meal was coming from. Or did they?

"I should be more like those ducks." She felt that she could say things like that to Parker. "Look! They are smiling. They are on the hunt half the time, but they come up smiling."

"That's not a smile."

"Yes, it is," she protested with laughter. "Look at the curve of that beak. That's a smile if I ever saw one. I wish I could smile like all the time. Just smiling – that would be nice."

"Don't you feel that you come up smiling?"

"No, I don't. Life is too hard sometimes."

But today was not hard. Today was an adventure. She felt the companionable silence behind her, saw the water dark and solemn beneath them, felt the warmth of the sun across her back, leaching in through the windbreaker, and she felt the goodness of it all, a new ember glowing deep inside herself in the fire pit of her soul.

Two hours downriver, she looked upward as they went underneath the Greenfield bridge, seeing the underside of the steel grid and the underside of cars passing above. She waved.

"You never viewed it from this perspective, did you?" Parker's voice was a tenor solo backed up with harmony from the bass vibrations of the steel. She shivered at the sound.

"No."

She got her first taste of whitewater a few more miles south as they rushed past Makepeace Island. She caught her breath at the excitement. Her eyes glowed. She heard a chuckle behind her.

"Just sit tight, and let me steer."

"Yes, Parker." She dutifully pulled her paddle up and hung on to the wales with both hands, enjoying the misty spray in her face.

". . . Indian story with that island. Before all the Indian troubles began in the French and Indian War, the settlers and the Indians met on that island for a pow wow." Parker's voice floated behind her.

"I bet you know the history of this entire area." Becky giggled.

"Of course. That's my job. . . . but it's damn interesting, too." He chortled deep inside himself. Facing front though she was, in her mind's eye Becky could see the blonde chest hairs rise up and down with that chortle. She liked it that he could laugh.

"Tell me more."

"You really want to know?"

"Sure! Give me the A tour, I want to know everything."

She suddenly was interested in everything – history, geography, biology, astronomy. Where had she been when those subjects were being taught in school?

She was disappointed to see the rocky landing at Wexford coming up. She knew that was where Parker had left his pickup truck in the parking lot ready for their return.

A pang of loss wrenched through her. At the end of the ride, she already was missing the beauty, the buoyancy, the blissfulness, as she and Parker lifted the canoe to lash it to the roof rack. But there was a real sense of accomplishment, too, as she settled into the passenger seat for the ride home. She had done it. She had been half the team that had brought the canoe down the river and, now, brought that canoe home. She felt a proprietary interest in every lashing that held the canoe in place. She grinned from ear to ear.

Back at the inn, the barbecue grill nurtured white-hot coals. Dave and Pamela readied the hamburgers and hot dogs. Daniel raced up and down on the browning grass, a one-man game of catch in progress. As soon as he saw Becky, he came running on chubby legs, ready to take his accustomed place on her hip.

But Parker would have none of it.

"Come on, young man," he shouted. "I'll teach you how to play baseball."

He took the Nerf bat that materialized from somewhere deep inside the pickup truck, handed it to Daniel, and the lesson began, lean, blonde 6-footer hovering over the toddler, showing him the proper batting stance. Becky grinned at the sight.

Later, over dishes, they sang folk songs to Pamela's guitar accompaniment. Becky took Daniel, who was nodding off in her arms, and headed upstairs. Without turning on a light, she found the crib and tucked him in. She heard the sounds of the guitar drifting up through the grate, curling around her, comforting her, making her glad to be at home in the serendipitous warmth of this inn, with these serendipitous friends.

Later, after Parker and his friends had left, Becky did not want to let the good feelings of the day go. She took a warm blanket, threw it around her shoulders and sat on the steps leading to the river, melding herself into the darkness of the riverbank, watching the fish jump in silvery splashes in the moonlight. She felt rather than saw the deer come down to drink. She counted four shadows among the untamed shrubbery downriver, and two of the shadows had faint white spots glimmering in the moonlight. Then she saw a moving stripe of white and held very still because she suspected that a skunk was out and about. She was amazed. She had never known there was so much life out here after dark.

Still sitting there at midnight, she saw a black bear come down on the opposite river bank for some fishing and a bath. Afterward, the lumbering beast clambered out of the water, and, shaking itself like a dog, made the water spray in a halo, every drop glinting silver in the light of the full moon. She sat up in wonder, knowing she had just seen one of the great sights of the universe.

There, in the moonlight before she decided to go inside to bed, Becky realized that she was happy, truly happy, a sensation that she had forgotten existed.

CHAPTER SEVEN

Visitation day was excruciating for Becky. Once a month she drove her old sedan, rattling and clanking through the curves, past the ravines and rises, up the mountain road to the Wilsons' home. The cedar-shingled, post-and-frame building with a huge glass prow front, had a view of the valley that left onlookers breathless.

Sometimes Becky wondered about the privacy issues of that glass front. The Wilsons had drapes, but they liked to keep them open so as not to spoil the view. People all the way across into New Jersey could see this house, could peer right into that glass-fronted living room. Never mind that these onlookers were miles away. That's what telescopes were for. Becky knew for a fact that there were observation telescopes on the mountains in New Jersey. You put quarters into a slot, turned a knob, and the machine came to life, giving magnified views of the lush farmland, busy towns, and rolling mountain slopes to the observer.

Occasionally she wondered if she could make an issue of this openness, of nude Daniel standing in the living room for all the world to see, take the Wilsons into court for child abuse, but then she decided her overactive imagination was simply running away with her. It probably was best to not bring up the Wilsons' house anyhow, because that would just emphasize the issue of their prosperity and her poverty.

Yes, you could definitely see the house from below. On shadowed moments, the A outline of the front appeared as a man-made triangular slash amid the mottled gray and green of stone and foliage on the ridge. Sometimes, though, a sharp flash of light caught Becky's eye as she was parking at the mall or driving on the interstate. Becky knew this flash was merely sunlight reflecting off that glass prow, but to her anxiety over Daniel, it was a call of alarm, even on the best day.

Today was definitely not a best day; she was driving upward for the monthly weekend visit proscribed for the Wilsons' months ago by a black-robed judge at the county courthouse. For the first nine months of Daniel's life, she had been breastfeeding, so the visits had lasted only two or three hours. Once he had been weaned, however, the visits went to one weekend a month. She delivered him to the Wilsons on Saturday morning and picked him up on Sunday evening.

From the beginning, she had said she'd do the driving. "If they want visitation, they should put the effort and expense into driving," her Legal Aid lawyer had advised her. Becky, however, did not want the prying eyes of these exacting grandparents looking into her life on a regular basis. Driving both ways gave her some privacy.

The flames of October's red and orange hardwood-leaf extravaganza were fading to a drab collection of brown and black pickup sticks – fallen logs and branches lying every which way amid the forest undergrowth. Even the creek looked drab today; the water was low; granite boulders angled upward breasting dark washes where brown leaves churned in the whirlpools of tannin-colored water.

Daniel was as clean as she could get him. Early this morning, she had boiled a potful of water and poured it into the claw-foot tub, adjusted the temperature with another potful of cold water, and bathed Daniel until he was clean. Even with a towel cushioning the bottom of the tub, Daniel, slippery with shampoo and soap, was a real handful as she scrubbed and rinsed. She was exhausted by the time he was clean, dry, and dressed.

Now she was glad of her effort. The boy she was handing over smelled like Johnson's baby shampoo. His sweat suit was a new purchase, second-hand from the Kiddie Exchange but spotlessly clean. He wore the new blue winter jacket. Becky had pondered over that jacket. October days were still pretty warm, but evenings were darn cool.

The usual knot formed in her stomach as she pulled into the Wilson's blacktop driveway. Take a deep breath, she instructed herself, and twice she pulled the air into the lower part of her lungs, contracting her diaphragm and lifting her chest to let all the under-used bronchioles and alveoli fill with oxygen, hoping to calm herself.

The doorbell made a melodic chime. Then, she could see shadows moving through the colored-glass window of the door. Finally, with an outward rush of warm air, the door opened. Jane Wilson stood there, mouth contracted to a frown as she scrutinized Becky, but her arms were greedy for the living, breathing treasure Becky was handing over. She smiled as she reached for Daniel.

"Mommy," Daniel whimpered. Becky felt his arms tighten on her neck.

"Here's Grandma," Becky offered bravely. "Grandma Jane."

He gave a tentative peep out from his hiding place on Becky's shoulder, and then, recognizing who it was, turned to his grandmother with an arm out for transfer.

Becky felt the shifting of weight, the lightening of her load, with a thud in the pit of her stomach.

Then, she handed over the diaper bag. The bag was only lightly loaded -- Mrs. Wilson had wisely outfitted her house with diapers and clothes for visits from Daniel – but Becky made sure he arrived with his own toothbrush, his nighttime bottle, his favorite stuffy, and his sippy cup.

"Here, there, Sweetheart. Aren't you warm in that jacket?" Mrs. Wilson cooed to him.

"I wanted to make sure he had the jacket in case it got cold."

"Umm," was the only reply.

"He's had his breakfast."

"Okay."

"You have my cell phone number if you need me."

"Yes."

"I'll pick him up at 6 tomorrow evening," Becky affirmed.

"Sure," said Mrs. Wilson, and then, the door was shut, and Becky walked back on the paving stones to her car amazed again that Mrs. Wilson managed to communicate so much hostility with so few words. She took another deep, calming breath before getting into the car to head down the mountain and into a long, lonesome weekend.

Becky did not, in fact, have a cell phone that worked as she discovered when she tried to call Barb to make plans for the evening. After she pushed send, the phone gave out its usual annoyed whine, and then a distorted human voice transmitted a garbled message before the transmission broke off into nothingness. Becky listened to the vast blankness for a moment, hoping against hope that a signal would connect, but no dice.

It wasn't just the location and signal or no signal, either. She drove around from the McDonald's parking lot to Wal-Mart, which was further from the mountain ridge and more open, but the phone would not connect to Barb's phone here, either. That mysterious voice seemed to be telling her something – something about billing. She bet she knew what the urgent but unintelligible message was. She hadn't paid her Verizon bill.

Vexed with herself, she drove into town. Barb, as usual, was behind the counter at Van Doren's Diner handing out plates of eggs and hash browns and pouring coffee. Barb was a bit taller than Becky and sturdy; she carried the weight of all those dinners with ease. This morning, she had her light brown hair tied in two neat braids framing her face, each falling into a curl on her uniformed shoulder. The braids gave her an innocent, sun-kissed, Bavarian look. Her polished fingernails were alternating yellow and orange, which, surprisingly, added to the Alps-maiden effect. Her smile, though, was wicked – as usual. Her cheeks curled up into knobs of pink. Becky smiled back.

"No Daniel?" Barb, noticing his absence, raised one eyebrow. Becky always marveled at Barb's flexible face.

"Nah. It's visitation weekend, and Parker's working. Wanna get together tonight?" Becky asked.

"Wadda you want to do?"

"Just hang out and talk."

Barb gave a thumbs up with her free hand.

"Sounds good! I get off at 3. Come for dinner; I've got a chuck roast in the frig."

"Great. I'll bring a video from the library."

Such simplicities made Becky's infrequent outings with her girl-friends thoroughly satisfying. She wouldn't be lonely with Barb to keep her company.

Becky spent the afternoon at the library. She read the New York Times and browsed the shelves until she found three books that interested her. Then, she settled into a comfortable armchair and read until it was time to check out. She drove directly to Barb's place, finding a parking space on the street. Barb's apartment was in the attic of a house in a quiet wooded area.

"We have to be tip-toe around," Barb reminded her. "My land-lord complains about the footsteps over his head."

"Then he shouldn't rent out his upstairs," Becky commiserated.

"I know, but that's the way it is," Barb apologized. "He wants the money but the quiet, too."

". . . can't have it both ways."

"You can think so if you're the landlord."

Later, the two women cooked a beef stew, and they ate the hearty meal with buttered Italian bread and red wine until they were stuffed. They talked about men and movies, and high school days and hopes for the future. Both were busy these days playing the young-adult survival game.

"So what movie did you bring?"

"'The Way We Were' – Robert Redford."

"Oh, yum. I'd like to see him come in for breakfast some morning."

"Me, too."

"Barbra Streisand's pretty good in this movie, too."

"Wrong sex for me."

"Yeh, but she's a good actress."

"That she is."

" . . makes good story."

"Sure does."

Becky and Barb agreed on almost everything. They had been in sync ever since they had first met on a September afternoon of their freshman year of high school. Becky was taking a pile of textbooks home to cover with the proscribed brown paper and was struggling with the load. When she tried to open the front door of the school, her purse caught on the door bar and dropped. Its contents went everywhere; pennies and barrettes, pens and paperclips, tissues and jelly beans spread in remarkable array across the exit way and were kicked and stepped on by students pressing from behind.

Becky was afraid to bend over to retrieve her property; she'd get trampled. A girl came to her rescue, standing in the middle of the flooding crowd, arms outstretched to block the surge, voice giving a commanding warning, until Becky, off balance because of the books she was carrying, could retrieve her scattered property. The girl was Barb, and they'd been best friends ever since.

Tonight was no different. They talked, giggled, and shared confidences for hours. Eventually, Barb threw Becky out.

"I've got to be at work at 6 a.m.," she reminded Becky. "I've got to get some sleep."

Becky drove back to the inn reluctantly. She did not relish being there all by herself listening to the inn as it settled and shifted in the night..

The books would keep her company, she thought. She hugged the one she was reading to her breast, but sometime in the middle of the night she awoke, stacked that book with the others and turned off the lamp on the bedside table. So much for getting a few more pages read before she fell asleep.

The next morning, she was impatient. She planned her day, but there simply were too many hours until 6 p.m. She had coffee and then ate; whipping up a tuna-salad sandwich used up a little bit of her nervous energy. Now what? She was too antsy to focus on the pages of the book.

She walked the length of the dining room and back. Then, she put on her coat and went outside. Seeing all the leaves waiting to be cleared from the parking lot, she got the rake and put some wild abandon into that effort.

Finally, with some relief, she realized the afternoon was half over, and she'd better get herself cleaned up before she interacted with Mrs. Wilson again. She repeated the boiling water and the claw-foot-tub routine of the morning before, except this time, she washed her own hair and body. When she was done, she smelled of shampoo and Irish Spring soap.

Brr! The bathroom was cold when you were undressed and wet, Becky realized. She'd have to remember this when bathing Daniel. She dried and put on clean clothes quickly, getting ready for her return trip to the Wilsons.

On the way, she stopped at the Exxon station at the edge of Greenfield where she told the attendant to add $20 worth of gas and handed him the crisp bill she had reserved for the purpose. Life certainly required some planning and some discipline, she mused as she watched the indicator rise to – almost – half full.

She was on the way to pick up Daniel, though, and she sang to herself – a little song of joy surging in her breast as she drove the mountain road. Evening was creeping over the landscape, but, in a few minutes, she'd have him back in her arms, into his car seat, heading back to their own home. She was eager for the warmth of his hug, the rhythmic breathing in the air space beside her, the rattle of the crib as he turned in his sleep. She'd not be lonesome tonight.

CHAPTER EIGHT

October blew to a bone-chilling finale. The gold was torn from the trees by rain and wind, and a winter landscape in lattices of gray and brown was revealed. Sitting in front of the Discovery channel, with its shifting patterns of multicolored light playing on her face, Becky decided that she and Daniel would do their Halloween rounds dressed as a mama and baby gorilla.

Mother gorillas take good care of their children, the wildlife program told her. A gorilla's babies are spaced about four years apart because it takes her that long to raise each one. On the other side of the motherhood coin are rabbits, she learned. Rabbits have litters and more litters in the expectation that some of the offspring, by the sheer force of their numbers, will survive to adulthood.

In another lifetime, Becky might have chosen to dress up as rabbits, cute and pink, with ribbons on their floppy ears, but solemnly now, in the glow of enlightenment, she saw how right it was that she and Daniel become gorillas-for-a-night.

Besides, gorilla costumes would be warm, a practical consideration in a season that was turning more frigid by the day.

So it was that she borrowed Barb's gorilla-head mask for herself and cleaned area thrift shops out of all fur-like material that could be used to stitch up the matching costumes. This was Daniel's first Halloween trick-or-treat, and she wanted to do it right, to set a bar they could rise to in future years.

One afternoon, she was struggling with needle and thread and fur creating gorillas when she heard the crunch of a large vehicle on the gravel, the rattle of a door opening, the tap, tap, tapping of a litter of footsteps coming across the gravel and onto the porch.

She leapt up to answer the door, but she was too slow. The main inn door opened, and, amid raucous chatter, a group of people entered without knocking

The first thing she saw was the huge, bloodied bandage wrapped around a head.

"Yes?" She was startled. "Don't you knock?" She clutched Daniel to her.

"Lou sent us."

"What do you mean, Lou sent you?" She arched her brow quizically, trying to look officious, like an innkeeper.

"We had a bus accident and needed a place to stay. Lou sent us over here." More than a dozen people were milling about behind the speaker.

"We were coming home from a Phish concert." A gawky brunette giggled. ". . . went off the road. Do you have anything to eat? I'm starved."

Becky's blood ran cold.

"The inn is not open." She shrugged her shoulders in rejection. Daniel clung to her in fear at the phalanx of strangers, sucking his thumb as he peeked out from behind her legs.

"But Lou said just come over and grab bedrooms and make ourselves at home. We don't need inn service -- just a place to stay." The blonde twirled a greasy lock of hair in her fingers. A shower would be needed, too, Becky realized.

Then, Becky saw the rest of the bandages, bruises, slings, Band-aids, crutches at the ready,

"Whatever happened to you guys, anyhow?" Becky was concerned for them despite her fright. "You look like a bunch of mummies."

"Bus accident. Nobody's hurt very bad, but our driver got arrested for drunken driving."

"Looks like the bus sitting out front to me." Her voice went dry with disbelief.

"I drove it over," said the broad-shouldered, blonde, blue-eyed Tyrolean type in front. "But I was taking a chance. Our driver is the only one with a commercial license, and we have to wait for him to get bailed out of jail before heading home."

Becky was sure she smelled the cloying scent of marijuana drifting out of the crowd.

"I'm Neal, and this is Lee."

"We're from Columbus, Ohio," a small, gray-faced girl piped up. "Oh, God, do I have a hangover. I need a bed."

Becky's gaze brushed across the Ohio State sweatshirt, stained with God knows what. She could not let this crew stay here without authorization from the owner himself. Their word on it was not good enough. She felt better working her way through the initial bewilderment to this understanding.

"I'll talk to Lou."

"Oh, thank you. Thank you."

They thought that meant yes. She thought that meant no.

Becky sighed. It was almost Halloween. The mummies of the fishing camp, that's what they were, come to haunt her.

The bus itself, taking up half the parking lot, was a fantasy of color, airbrushed with a flower-child abandon. The front half featured jagged leaves consorting with magenta flowers heavy with the poisons of a thousand humid jungles. Creeper vines constricted the burgeoning mass into a bus-like shape. Toward the rear, a rainbow leapt skyward, hopeful of completion around a corner, but, as it made the turn to the back of the bus, it blended into a multi-colored sunset scene that waved a farewell as the bus sped away from the viewer. Through it all, the animals peeped out, two by two, elephants and giraffes, lions and bears, anteaters and antelope, reveling in their jungle haunts.

The dent in the driver's side of the bus, the dent that had brought them all here, merely looked like a cave, a dark and mysterious depth worth exploring, some animal's home, a silent haven in the middle of the jungle frenzy.

Becky stared in awe at this vivid palette of the passenger bus dropped down into the middle of the browning landscape of the Duck Point Inn's parking lot. Her faded blue sedan paled to conservative insignificance beside the bus's exotic splendor.

"We should charge admission to the ark."

"What? Oh! Umm!" Neal fumbled, unsure about the nature of Becky's sarcasm.

Circling to the front, Becky saw a concentric pattern of shattered glass in the windshield.

"There," Neal pointed. "That's where my head hit."

"How'd you end up there? Weren't you in a seat?"

"I was standing up telling a joke to the assembled audience. . . went ass over teakettle."

She clucked in mock sympathy. "It's a wonder you didn't get killed."

She grimaced at the macabre image the thought of the accident brought to mind.

"Who owns this bus, anyhow? Some bus company?"

"Actually the driver and his brother own the bus – make a living, such as it is, putting together bus trips to concerts and such for university students."

"I see. Well, I'm gonna call Lou."

Her cell phone was still on the unpaid list. In order to call Lou, she had to drive to town; Barb would let her use hers.

She was worried though. The sedan was on empty and she'd need to stop at the Exxon. At night the Tiger Mart was a scary place with gangly teenagers, sweatshirt hoods pulled forward to hide their faces, hanging out in the ice-blue glow of the overhead lights. Now, though, in late afternoon, it should be less scary. She knew she must go right away, though, before the daylight faded. She was angry at using her precious cash reserve for this. Still, she had no choice.

The bald tires spun on the leaves, damp with autumn moisture. Patience, she told herself. Patience. Tomorrow there would be more raking trying to keep this incline free of leaves. Maybe some of those jokers could even help her -- their presence might not be an entirely negative thing -- but tonight she had to talk to Lou, so she guided the sedan, slow and steady, creaking and sputtering, up the road, heading for the diner. Daniel, thank God, fell asleep in his car seat in the back.

"Why, Sweetheart," Lou said after she had explained the situation. "I am just trying to do a good deed here. One of those young men is the nephew of a good friend – goes to Ohio State – trying to get back to school – distraught that he is missing classes."

"If he's so distraught about classes, how come he took a bus trip to a rock concert in New York state?"

"Now, now. A little charity, please. Nobody expected this accident to happen."

"How long do they expect to be here?"

"Oh, a few days." The telephone line crackled and sputtered in her ear.

"I do not have the food to feed this crew for a few days. I do not have the food to feed them breakfast, as a matter of fact. It is almost the end of the month, and my SNAP card is empty." She pulled her new blue parka tighter around her, warding off the wind whistling up the highway. She could hear Daniel, awake now, screaming his impatience in the car.

"There, there, Sweetheart. They should be buying their own groceries; that was our deal – it was not to cost me any money. But, if it'll make you feel any better, I'll go shopping first thing in the morning."

"Yes. Good idea." You'd better, she thought. Not to cost me anything either.

Dialing again, she roused Parker from sleep.

"Please come and stay at the inn," she begged, explaining the situation. "I need you."

Trust.

That was something she had never thought about until this moment. The past two years she had lived a life of mistrust, but make do, take what you had to take for survival, and watch your back. That was the way of her relationship with Lou. That was the way she had felt about Mac MacGreavy. That was the way she now felt about the wayfarers back at the inn. But she knew that the phone call to Parker had been different.

Trust. She was almost afraid to confront this brand-new feeling for fear it would not be real. But when Parker showed up just a few minutes after her arrival back at the inn, she knew that trust was the core of her feeling for him. She wasn't sure if that was good or bad.

She installed Parker in the bedroom next to hers, letting the newcomers straggle down the hallway into whatever other accommodations were available, and, when she locked her door that night, both knob lock and bolt, she knew that she was not locking it against Parker Sims.

CHAPTER NINE

Becky awoke to the sound of a recorder playing a melody. "Bridge Over Troubled Waters" spun its way through the morning, curling up through the grate and tickling her feet where they stuck out from underneath the quilt. The melodic sound of the recorder gave way to squabbling voices .

"I wanna watch *Jersey Shore.*"

"No. The rest of us want cartoons!"

The frenetic dialogue and music of Scooby-Do followed. By this time, Becky was awake. Why they were right underneath her, making themselves at home in front of her television!

Should she throw them out?

Was that part of her job as caretaker here? To treat these newcomers as the vandals and trespassers that Lou was worried about, or did they, in fact, with Lou's permission to be here, have as much right to the rooms below as she? Did she in saying okay last night take on the job of innkeeper instead of caretaker? Becky's brain had difficulty being objective here. This new development meant a lot of work and a lot of uncertainty. She had not signed on for either.

She heard a soft knock on her door and unlocked it to let in Parker.

The ranger, looking official in his khaki uniform, neat black handgun strapped to his waist, said a farewell.

"I have to go to work, but it looks okay to me. They're just out of place and out of time."

"What do you mean?"

"Woodstock is about 50 miles back and 50 years ago."

"But Lou has given his okay for them to stay, so what can I do?"

"Actually, they look harmless enough. Just don't let them eat you out of house and home."

She grimaced.

He laughed. "Gotcha where it hurts, did they?"

Her face fell in dismay,

"I'll call Lou – in a semi-official capacity, if you want."

"Just tell him to get some food down here."

"Sure thing. But I think they are just a bunch of college kids stranded, like they say they are. I'll check out the bus driver situation for you though. Maybe I can prod things along a bit there."

He waved and headed off down the stairs, hiking boots clumping at every step.

She thrust her feet into her $9.97 fuzzy slippers and followed the scent of coffee down to the bar, where Neal poured her a robust cup of Columbian – they had found her private stock of coffee – and, with a flourish, served her a plate of French toast, which only exacerbated her anxieties.

"Good thing you had plenty of bread with all these people," Neal commented, and her stomach took a flip flop like the French toast upside down in the pan.

Daniel dug in like a champ. He loved French toast. Both fists and his face were soon sticky with butter and syrup. Becky tapped the handle of her fork on the table in exasperation. She was not sure she could eat a bite.

After breakfast, Becky took a whistling-in-the-dark detour past the shadowed alley of her fear and peeked around at the crowd, lounging in varying poses of recline around the bar and the dining room.

Closest to her was a woman chic with a white sheet wrapped around her body and a white cast from fingers to shoulder on her right arm. "Mary Ellen," she introduced herself in a plaintive treble voice. Mary Ellen seemed to be paired with Clifford, who had a gashed arm stitched and bandaged from elbow to shoulder. His good right arm often wrapped around Mary Ellen fondly, and they laughed in unison. Becky was sure they were a twosome.

Cliff really needed three arms, though, Becky decided. He also had a laptop, but between the bandages and Mary Ellen, no hand was left to work the keyboard. He kept fighting off the others who all wanted to "borrow – just for a moment" the laptop.

"I want to play *Second Life*. Do you think I could use it for that?"

"Don't you have Wi-fi here?"

"How about a game of Solitaire?"

"Is this the only computer we've got? What is wrong with us?"

"I've got my iPod, but it won't work for some reason."

"I'm not sure we have access to the Internet," Becky told them. "I don't even get a cell phone signal."

"We noticed."

"What is this place anyhow? The backside of the moon?"

They'd only been here a half a day and the complaints had already begin.

"I'm Lisa," said the ash blonde with the recorder, waving at Becky before going back to her playing. Lisa seemed to be reasonably whole, with no visible injuries. She sat cross-legged in orange tights and pink off-one-shoulder tee shirt. Her feet were bare, and the nail polish on her toenails matched the tee shirt. She closed her eyes as she played.

Beyond the bulwark of pink and orange was an array of injuries, bandaged knees, casts, legs propped up on pillows, bandaged elbows, gauze-wrapped heads, ice packs – and, yes, they were paired off in twos, guys and girls hugging, comforting, girls and girls with their heads together gossiping – except for Neal Hamilton who seemed, if anything to be paired with the fireplace. He had taken on its stoking as his own personal destiny.

"How long do you think you'll be staying?" There! The question was asked. Her voice sounded thin and reedy to her, coming from far away, with a breathless pause at the question mark.

"Not too long we hope," piped in Clifford.

"Actually, some people made other arrangements. They flew home or something. This is the group that decided to rest up a few days before deciding what to do next." Neal Hamilton turned away from the fire for a moment, standing imperiously over the reclining crowd.

". . . or those who didn't want to go home," added Lisa.

Neal wrinkled his nose and made a shushing face at her.

"All those who had to be at work or at class Monday morning took up their crutches and walked. They pulled out their plastic and flew home, deserting us for the rigors of real life." Lisa would not be shushed.

"Don't you guys have credit cards or something that could get you on your way?"

"No." The word came as a grumble from underneath quilts, behind pillows.

"I'm flunking two courses," piped in an overweight woman with two-tone pink hair. Personally, I'm glad of a good excuse to start the semester all over again."

Neal, taking stage front, waved his arms outward in an expansive gesture of inevitability. The travelers all laughed.

Becky did not laugh. She could feel her saliva glands spew lemon into her mouth, tart and constricting. Her lips pursed. Her face squinched.

"Relax, Darling. Relax," Neal urged her.

When had she become his darling? No thanks.

"We'll help," the small, gray-faced girl whispered. She was holding a towel full of ice cubes to her head.

Sure you will, Becky thought. How is anybody supposed to help around here with casts up to their chins? As for Neal, with that head injury I bet he passes out first time he tries to do something.

As the day wore on, though, Becky found it hard to sustain her anger. Except for Neal, who grated on her nerves, she felt oddly comfortable with these people – hapless, harmless, homeless, just like herself. This inn was big, and she had been getting lonely with no one to talk to but Daniel.

Through the morning, Lisa sang softly, an old folk ditty about October being a golden month. ". . . coins in your pocket, um, um, um," and the crowd curled up in twosomes while the fireplace – stoked with a small mountain of Becky's wood – poured its heat out against the chill of the coming winter. She ought to be terrified, outraged, she knew, but, as the afternoon wore on, she could not conjure up that emotion no matter how hard she tried.

Party! Party! Party!

The crowd had discovered the bar stock, and, no matter how meager the selection really was, if they weren't fussy about what they were drinking, there was enough alcohol to sustain the raucousness for several days.

Neal would sing, "Engine No. 9, leaving on Columbus line," and the whole group would laugh uproariously and join in.

"All aboard!"

"You're making that up! Surely there is no song like that one."

"Yes, there is," he snickered and stumbled. ". . . a variation on a theme." Hiccup.

Daniel shrank from them, shrinking behind her legs and then crawling into a cupboard behind the bar.

Finally, Becky grabbed Daniel under one arm and climbed the stairs to hide in her room. She tried to focus on her Halloween preparations. The crowd below was a constant flow of excited conversation and high-pitched laughter, the clink of glasses and the scrape of chairs. Like the sound of water lapping against rocks at the river's edge, the noise of the partying become a given throughout the inn. It could not be turned off.

All Hallow's Eve had finally arrived. To warn or not to warn? That became her question as she readied the gorilla debut. Finally, assessing the depths of communal drunkeness, she decided she'd better warn them all of the impending gorilla appearance. Even so, having told them all about the costumes, there were gasps as she and Daniel appeared on the balcony. Cheers followed her as she crept tremulously down the stairs past the antlered heads. She felt assurance firm up her backbone.

"You are a gorilla, Girl," she told herself, as she gave a stage wave to the assembled drunken patients, girding up her courage as she went out past the jungle-painted bus.

"You look real natural, posed in front of that bus," Neal called to her. He was lounging in the doorway, an angled figure leaning against the door jamb. She turned to look at the bus. A pair of gorillas looked back at her.

"Heh," she laughed at the joke as she sidled past the bus, going to her own sedan.

"Bring us back some candy!"

"Yeh. We've got the munchies."

Humph, Becky grumbled to herself. If they thought she was going to do their trick-or-treating for them, they had another think coming.

Becky and Daniel were a big hit in the Greenfield residential neighborhoods. Mama-gorilla Becky, walking on sidewalks, climbing steps to front doors with baby-gorilla Daniel, came back to the inn with a pillowcase half full of candy and memories of lighted doorways where suburban matrons posed imperiously above the open mouths of candy-greedy goblins. It had been good fun.

How different could her resident crowd of goblins be, really? In a burst of generosity, she had worked the front door bells for an extra hour to have enough candy to share with them.

She arrived back at the inn to find that Lou had come and gone, a phantom in the Halloween twilight, two days late, but leaving bags of groceries and removing the remains of the liquor stock. She was immensely grateful for both actions.

The inn returned to its status of hospital ward, but this time the inhabitants were nursing giant-size hangovers in the shadowed corners of the dining room, and Tylenol became the drug of choice.

The supply of pot seemed to go on forever. Day or night – it didn't matter.

"Look, guys. You really have to keep the smoking to the main room. When you smoke in the bar room, it comes up through the grate, and I've got a kid up there."

Neal seconded her plea. "Sure, thing. We don't want to get the kid high."

Every time Becky came downstairs, though, somebody was passing a joint around. They'd take a drag, hold it deep for a moment, and exhale gray smoke. Then the joint went on to the next person until it was smoked down to the last quarter of an inch. Sometimes they'd pull out a glass pipe and fill the small bowl with a brown, shredded material set afire with a lighter. The pipe would be passed in the same way, person to person around the room. The whole group was glassy-eyed, sitting in their circle swaying back and forth, leaning against each other for support.

They offered Becky a drag every time she entered the room, but she always shook her head with a firm no. Daniel was too big a responsibility for her to play those kinds of games, she felt. This inn wasn't exactly kid-proofed; she needed to keep her wits about her.

Lisa, playing her recorder, seemed to be less stoned than the rest. Besides, she had a big mouth. Becky wondered if she could get some reliable information from her.

"Lisa, where is all this pot coming from?"

Lisa brushed her pale hair back from her milky face, and, for a moment, Becky could see pale, gray eyes unsheltered by lashes. Lacy white eyebrows furrowed into the center of her face as she responded.

"Tim. Tim has it. He had a whole backpack full. He was selling rolled joints at the concert, hoping to make a killing, but he had a lot left over."

"I see. Are they planning on smoking it all?"

"I think so."

"How long will that take them?"

"Depends on how many joints they roll a day."

Becky took a deep breath. "Well, at the rate they're going, how long will it take them to smoke up this supply?"

"Maybe until Spring."

Becky lay her forehead on her fist. Spring!

Then, she began to worry about the amount of marijuana present in the inn. The backpack described by Lisa was enough to draw some serious jail time for a dealer charge.

. . . and it's not like they didn't have a law enforcement official going up the down the stairway to the bedrooms on a regular basis. How far did Parker take his law-enforcement responsibility? The stoneheads apparently kept an eye on his comings and goings, and the cigarettes passed around while he was present at the inn were of the Camel Gold variety. So far he had ignored the occasional leftover whiff of cloying sweetness. Had it even dawned on him that there was this much pot stashed somewhere in the inn? Of course he had. You'd have to be dumb, dumber, dumbest to miss it, and Parker was anything but dumb.

He could bring child services down on their heads, too. Becky didn't think he would do that – she felt he had made a personal commitment to their well-being -- but she got sick at the thought of what would happen if a child-welfare social worker showed up here.

Most of all, though, she worried about Daniel himself. She covered the heat grate with a rag rug. That cut off most of the smoke, but also most of the heat. The bedroom got even colder than before. Despite this barrier, she knew Daniel was getting some of this pot smoke, and even a little bit in his growing body and brain was too much for her. She had to get him out of here – but how?

With the beginning of November, Becky took another $20 and tucked it away with the bills in the back of her purse where they would be unseen, not tempting her to splurge on cookies or M&Ms. Such discipline is good for the figure, too, she told herself gamely. That brought her little stash up to $270.

One day Becky came upon Neal gazing steadfastly at the photograph of Babe Ruth with his string of enormous fish.

"Hey, look, Becky. This inn used to be for fishermen. Now it is for Phish-ermen, Ha Ha! Get it?"

Becky chuckled. She had to admit that she "got it." It was pretty funny, actually. She joined in the laughing.

The joke swept through the group, and, amid general chortling and knee-slapping, they adopted the name for themselves.

"We're the Phishermen of the Duck Point Inn," Neal sang off key. He pranced across the floor picking up a rollicking tune.

"I went to a darn good party,

Had a drink of darn fine rum, . . . "

He spread his hands wide in mock theatrical display. The music bounced up and down.

"Oh, god. Stop! You're making it sound like *The Pirates of Penzance*."

"Neal, shut up. If you're going to sing heavy metal, please make it sound like heavy metal."

". . . but it's all forgotten now

." His voice rang into a treble on the word "all."

They booed him to a silence.

Lisa picked up her recorder and began to play a tune. Soon several voices had joined together in another song.

"Di di do do."

They found a three-part harmony on the repeats.

"Time runs faster, faster, faster . . ."

"Yeh, that's more like it," somebody remarked with satisfaction.

"In my view an eagle, black against the sky. . ." Cliff's voice rose into a pleasing solo on this line.

"I'll be the eagle." Tim stood and, pretending he was soaring, stumbled across the dining room tangling his feet in quilts and crashing with a thud onto Maria's shoulder and a roll into her lap. He nuzzled the mottled fabric covering her legs.

"Umm, umm, good."

"Hey, that hurt," Maria complained, pushing him away. "Get lost, you pervert."

"Yeh, yeh, Tim. Smoke another one."

He rolled over again, bumping this time into Mary Ellen.

"Stop that."

"Can't we even sing like sane adults," complained Cliff – and so another shining moment of music with the Phishermen came to an end. Somebody produced a large bag of potato chips that soon was being passed around amid wantings and whinings from the crowd, hands outstretched in heartfelt supplication for the salty, greasy food. To Becky it looked like a rendition of Hell from the Middle Ages.

Where did they get potato chips? she wondered. Those voluminous backpacks were a never-ending source of surprise.

November opened frosty and chill. With a new deposit on her SNAP card, Becky went shopping,

She lugged her own groceries up to her room, and hid them in the armoire.

"Am I being selfish about this?" She asked Parker.

"Not at all. You can't let them use all your resources. Do you want to move out? That might be the best thing."

"Where am I going to go?"

A glimmer of hope that Parker might come to her rescue and open up his home tugged at Becky. She lifted her face hopefully to him.

"Here! I'm going to give you a cell phone that works."

She pursed her lips in disappointment.

"I do not want you down here without a phone. I'll let you have one of mine for the time being."

"We don't get very good reception down here in this valley. Most of the time, nobody can get a signal."

"Even so, it's better to have a phone. You can drive up to the road if you need to."

He flipped the phone up in his hand, showing her how it worked. As he turned it on, the colors flashed across the screen and a jolly jingle sounded.

"Thanks. So you think I am in danger here?"

"Never can tell. One thing I have learned about this river, though – people get up here and they are on vacation, in another world. Most people just have fun in that other world, but for some people the rules are suspended. Those are the ones you have to watch out for."

"Okay. Thanks. I guess you know a lot more about this river than just the history and wildlife."

"My job, Hon. My job. . . . and, speaking of my job, I've got to go to work."

He gave a wave as he left.

The lodge was never silent. Nights, when she was lying in bed listening, fascinated Becky.

Close at hand, of course, the sound of Daniel's breathing filled the bedroom. She often listened for that breathing; slow and even, it spoke to her of health and well-being. Daniel was safe and fed and sleeping. Contentment bloomed with the sound of that night-time breathing. She felt satisfied that she had brought them successfully through to the end of another day.

Farther away, though, the building itself talked to her. Each individual building has its own set of sounds, she'd learned. Now, she listened carefully, making the acquaintance of the peculiarities of the inn. The rafters creaked and groaned both day and night. Sometimes Becky looked upward to make sure the structure was holding together. She pictured the shingled roof sliding off like the top of the doll houses she'd played with as a child; it would lie upside down on the riverbank while some giant child would reach in a pudgy giant hand to adjust the placement of the furniture or change the clothing on the dolls.

When the wind blew down from the north the whole building shook, and the antique striated glass rattled in the paper-dry window frames. On nights like that, Becky piled on the blankets and prayed for morning; she was never warm enough when the Hudson Bay express brought chill that penetrated every crack.

Overhead, the squirrels gamboled in the attic, racing and thudding, squeaking and mewing, scratching and chewing. The squirrels played and they fought. They mated. They squealed at each other. They rolled acorns across the vast expanse. At nighttime, lying in bed, listening to their goings-on, Becky came to realize they had a whole domestic and communal life up there, a whole other reality existing in the parallel universe of the attic.

Now that there were other human beings living in the inn, the downstairs environs were just as noisy, even in the darkest night. She heard footsteps in every corner of the building, brushing like fine sand-paper on the bare wood of the floors. Steps on the stair risers sounded like thunder. The kitchen door squeaked, and then squeaked again and again as it swung back and forth. The cupboard doors banged, and the refrigerators gave forth huge gasps of air when opened. Then there were the constant snufflings and coughings and turnings and complainings. She heard the crackling of food wrappers. She heard the moanings of sex.

She even fancied she heard the suck of breath intaking a puff from a pot pipe.

. . . and when somebody slammed a door, the crack of it sounded like thunder rolling down the gorge, with the skies enraged, the clouds roiling with nature's anger, rain thudding like spears thrown from the heavens, and the earth and the river provoked to a dark-hearted fury.

CHAPTER TEN

"**A**ll right, everybody. Dig deep. We got to get some food."

Becky sat up with an ear-to-ear smile, forgetting the Legos she had been playing with Daniel. She knew there was nothing left of Lou's donations. She knew they had polished off all the cartons of snacks from the fishermen's store and all the Halloween candy. She had been afraid they were going to start eating from her precious supplies next. However, with this call, the answer to her prayers was in view. They were going to buy their own groceries.

"I want pizza," said the lanky brunette.

"No, no pizza. There are 18 of us – 20 with Becky and Daniel – we have to make our resources last. I think we should go to the grocery store and get food to cook -- much cheaper." Neal Hamilton, long hair askew with static electricity, was taking charge, as usual, "Everybody cough up ten bucks."

"Ten bucks!"

"Neal is right. We should get stuff to make spaghetti and such."

A flurry of hoorays came from the assembled crowd, followed by the rustle of billfolds and the clink of change.

"I haven't got ten bucks."

"Well, then, give me what you've got." Neal's voice was firm. "We've got to eat."

Becky smiled her gratitude at him. Good. They were taking the weight of this away.

"If we plan it right, we should be able to eat for a dollar a day."

"I'm not sure we can cut it down to that little. You're dreaming."

"Well, do the best you can."

"Tim has money."

"No, I don't."

"What happened to all that pot money?"

For a moment they squabbled over Tim's alleged affluence. Then, the bills started to appear.

Money collected, Neal slipped his rumpled windbreaker over his Phish concert sweatshirt and turned to Becky.

"Would you drive?"

"Drive?" Her smile fell away.

"Yes. I don't think I should take that bus out. I will get a ticket for sure."

The resentment froze in her throat again, clogging her airway with the taste of bile. No matter how you sliced this loaf of bread, how you divided this pie, there was weight on her shoulders, a weight she had never asked for and did not want.

A tall girl sidled into the kitchen, her mouth pursed and her shoulders hunched.

"I can cook. I'll help you here."

"Really?"

"Sure. I'm Jackie. What are you making today?"

"Vegetable soup with keilbasi. You can help me peel and chop, and – thanks."

"You're welcome." Her lips twitched into a smile.

Jackie was tall, much taller than a woman should be, even seated, and when she stood , Becky could see the height was in her thighs, which splayed outward, like those of a young colt still unsure of how to hold itself upright. Her pelvis tilted forward, and her knees rotated with every step.

Becky felt very small, miniscule, beside this height. For a moment she looked upward into the unfamiliar face, wondering, but the smile reassured her.

Becky smiled back at her.

"Is there a chopping board?"

"Here."

". . . and where's the garbage?"

"There."

The kitchen soon echoed with the rhythmic chop of the knife slicing its way through celery and onions. Becky, looking sideways from the corner of her eye, marveled at the long, thin hands working over the chopping board. She'd never seen hands with such length. The hands were awkward. They did not seem to move in the same way Becky expected hands to move, but they certainly did an efficient job. The pile of chopped vegetables was growing into a mini mountain.

"The soup is started in that big pot on the stove. Just toss all the vegetables in."

"What are you using for the base?"

"I boiled the chicken carcasses and added canned tomato."

Then Becky turned from peeling the potatoes and saw that a third figure had lined up at the counter. Lisa -- that's who the third, silent but efficient, cook was. Becky recognized her by the single pale blonde pigtail lying against the bright pink sweatshirt.

"Hey, aren't you cold?"

Lisa had pink flip flops on her bare feet, and her toes were pale blue.

"Sure am! I really don't have anything else, but it's actually warmer getting up and about, doing things. It gets the blood flowing."

She ran in place for a moment, and then bent to the left and to the right.

"I've got a spare pair of bedroom slippers you can wear if you want."

"Thanks. That would be helpful."

Becky surprised herself with this unbridled generosity. It felt amazingly good. She could afford to be generous over this. She knew she had plenty of warm gear for her feet. She had adequate sneakers, fuzzy slippers, and plenty of socks. The slippers she had offered were foot-warmer socks with a hard plastic sole and knit material that pulled halfway up the leg. Lisa would be a lot warmer with them on. What a difference adequate resources make, Becky realized. Everything was relative. She could afford to loan, or even to give, these slippers to Lisa. She prayed for a world with adequate resources so she could go on being a generous person. What a paradox! To want so you could give it all away.

"No problem."

"I'd better wash my hands if I'm going to help."

Lisa moved to the sink and took off her pink mitts, cheap knit mittens with the fingers cut away, and Becky saw the ring. For a moment, Becky's breath strangled in her esophagus. Becky had grown up in a household that, while it couldn't necessarily afford everything, thought it singularly important, a cultural one-upmanship, to distinguish the very expensive genuine article from the fake. She knew how to tell a diamond from glass, and the diamond on Lisa's finger was definitely of the genuine variety.

Jackie, too, did a double-take.

"Hey, that ring could get us all home."

"Wow! Nice!" Becky held on to the vowels, lengthening the words.

Lisa saw them both looking. She shook her hands and finished drying them on a cotton terry dish towel.

"Paste." The word was a single flat note in an otherwise silent kitchen.

I bet, thought Becky, but she decided it was not her business. Let Lisa pass off this carat-plus stone as a simulation. It probably was safer for her that way. Becky, certainly, would not wear a many-thousand dollar gem in the many dubious situations she had been through in the previous two years. Probably, Lisa felt the same way.

"Keep the mitt on, girl. Better yet, put the ring on a chain around your neck where you can keep it out of sight at all times."

Lisa turned away, but not before Becky saw the blush creep up her throat and cheeks.

While Lisa's ring was a real revelation, all in all, the group was starting to sort itself out into individuals. Some of it was good, and some of it was bad.

Neal took the role as leader because he was gregarious, Becky realized. His mouth was always open with something to say. Cliff often made more sense, though. Becky soon learned to wait for the quiet second opinion before agreeing with anything they proposed. She realized she needed to stop thinking of the group as one amorphous mass and find the individuals within. They really were very different from one another.

The small, gray-faced girl was named Lee. She was not hard to distinguish from the crowd because she lay on the window seat all day long. Her vague lethargy was not due to use of recreational drugs, Becky soon realized, but due to real illness.

"I'm running out of my meds," she announced one day as the dinnertime bowls of red-bean and ground-turkey chili were being filled..

"Meds?"

"Yes, I really need to see a doctor." A pregnant pause followed.

"Meds for what?" Becky was wary. Meds – or the lack thereof – were the last thing she needed.

"You're not going to go berserk on us, are you? You're not going to attack us all with a knife in the middle of the night."

"Of course not. What do you think I am? A nut or something?"

"Well, what are these meds for?"

"I have an ulcer." Lee's indignation arced across the room. "I take medication for that, and I take Vitamin B12 capsules for the anemia. Both prescriptions are almost gone."

Becky looked at Neal.

". . . better do something, Neal."

"We don't have any money for a doctor."

". . . just take me to the emergency room at the hospital. They have to treat me, even without money, even without insurance."

"Who says?"

"They usually do; I've done it before. They chalk it up to charity care. All hospitals have a slush fund for us deadbeats – and, by the way -- whoever's shopping, my ulcer needs better food than this."

She gestured at the chili in her bowl.

This time, Neal spoke up.

"What's wrong with that food?"

"It's spicy, for one thing – spice is death on an ulcer -- and it's almost all beans. I don't like beans. I need food with iron in it, like beef steak and spinach salads."

"Sorry! The kitchen is all out of beef steak and spinach salad." Neal's mouth twisted into a frown and he stomped around the dining room in high indignation. "If you don't like the food, shop and cook it yourself."

Finally, he sat down and began to eat his own hot and spicy bowlful of chili – lots of red beans and tomato sauce flavored with a little ground turkey, as Lee had just so acerbically pointed out.

"Here, we have some saltines to go with that," Jackie offered trying to change the subject..

Becky took Daniel in one arm and her own personal serving of tonight's stretching-the-money, one-pot meal in the other hand and exited up the stairs for some peace and quiet while she dined.

Lee returned to her malaise on the window seat, adjusting the throw pillows to suit her back and the dirty wool blanket to suit her front. With her leg splayed out in faux sleep, the seat was full, and nobody else could share the cushioned expanse.

CHAPTER ELEVEN

Someone made a wooden plaque, painted it pink and blue, decorated it with hearts and flowers and hung it over the old-fashioned, stained enamel sink.

"Becky's Kitchen."

Becky wondered just when that miraculous transformation had come about.

Had it been with the western eggs or the spaghetti with meat sauce? Or perhaps the 79-cent-a-pound-when-bought-in-quantity chicken with rice?

Of one thing she was sure, though. She was getting tired of cooking for 20. Sure, the wayfarers had worked up a schedule for chores – for those who could work, that is – and she had plenty of help in the cavernous kitchen; some cooked and all helped with the washing up, but they all looked to her for direction. She was the planner and the guiding force. She was the menu maker and the shopping-list director.

Now, though, Neal Hamilton was having difficulty shaking any more money out of their pockets for groceries. They were running out of funds and scraping the bottoms of purses and backpacks for stray quarters and dimes.

"I wanna go home." Nancy burst into tears.

Great idea, seconded Becky silently.

"Why don't you just go?"

"I have no money. I can't walk to Ohio."

"Neal ought to crank up that bus and get it on the road, get you all home. I'll talk to him."

"Don't tell them I was crying, please. They'll make fun of me. I came out here in the kitchen to hide. I don't want them to know I am so upset over this."

"Okay. I'll keep you out of it."

She accosted Neal, though. "It's time to get this show on the road."

"What! Aren't you happy with us here?" His mouth turned down in a grimace, his eyes became black olive pits of astonishment.

"Aren't you guys missing classes or something."

"We've been gone too long already." He turned his hands outward in a gesture of inevitability. "Most of them figure the semester is lost – those that care anyhow."

Her insides twisted with jealousy at the thought of the lost semester, the classes they were missing, the college opportunities they were throwing away. She was astonished at herself, at the depth of this sudden, unheralded desire. She gasped for breath as the realization swept over her.

Neal interpreted her gasp as extreme irritation over their presence. He bounded into the dining room, leaving the kitchen doors swinging a hyperactive staccato behind him.

"We must make Becky happy," he shouted to the mob lying in various states of leisure in front of the roaring fire.

Terry looked up from his book. Susan stretched her cast-clad limbs. Sally yawned.

A few minutes later Becky looked out the window to see Neal chopping wood, sinews straining at the effort, and a dozen people, a colony of ants at work, restocking the wood pile. She put her coat on and went outside to join the group.

"Are you sure that's a good idea?" she asked him, reluctant to stop the enterprise but fearful of the consequences. "I mean with a head injury and all that."

"Nah. I'm not concussed. It's just stitches."

Someone made another wooden plaque, this time green and orange, decorated with an axe, and hung it over the woodpile.

"Becky's Woodpile."

At least they were making an effort.

Day or night meant nothing to the Phishermen, and card games or impromptu songfests were apt to spring up at any moment of the 24 hours. At first, Becky was annoyed with this lack of schedule. Daniel needed to sleep, and she was afraid the rowdiness would wake him. Then, she got used to the bodies sprawled on cushions in the dining room and the bar, to the games, to the noise.

"Now I propose a contest," Neal said one day. "Who is the prettiest woman in the room?"

"What kind of a question is that, Neal? You trying to get us killed?"

"Of course, it was no matter that the men whispered their opinions in corners every day. None of them wanted to alienate the women by even admitting that they had secret, sly opinions on the subject of pulchritude. Neal would open up this explosive question to the entire group.

It's really not a fair question." Cliff was the reconciliator of the group. "The girls all have different things that are special. Maria has spectacular hair, for example, and Jackie has magnificent eyes."

Maria and Jackie both smirked.

"And, besides – everybody's idea of beauty is different."

"No, not at all. Listen, everybody. Listen up."

The buzzings came to a halt as everybody turned their attention to Neal. The men looked dubious, and the women retained a certain, suspicious glint in their eyes.

"I am proposing that fate settle this question, for once and for all. I know how to select Miss Phish Bus Trip, and I will personally see that the honoree gets included in this year's OSU yearbook."

". . . how you gonna do that?"

". . . by bedding the editor. She'll be putty in my hands when I get done with her."

Eyebrows were raised around the room. Mouths pursed.

"Yeh, sure."

"Why don't we propose that the 'most beautiful woman' will be the one who goes through the swinging doors to the kitchen next."

A silence fell around the room as the implications of Neal's statement were digested.

"But, Neal. The women are all here, listening to what you said."

He smiled wickedly. The expression on his face was worthy of Jack Nicholson.

"Exactly."

He held the smile as the rustling began. Jackie was getting to her feet as if it were the most natural thing in the world to do. Lee rolled over from her back to her knees, preparing to rise from the window seat. Maria sidled along a wall. Nancy leapt up from a dining chair, startled that she had been so slow to action.

"Think I'll get a snack!"

The four of them collided at the swinging doors, arms akimbo, legs atangle, shoulders blocking the entryway.

"Me first."

"No, me."

They glared at each other. Maria pulled her fist back.

"Now, ladies. Please!"

Becky was frantic. She had never envisioned a brawl among this bunch. She leapt up to try to defuse the situation,

Neal erupted in peals of laughter.

"Do we have a photo finish? Yes, surely, there is a problem at the finish line." Neal was gloating.

"Oh, shut up, Neal," Jackie sneered. "You make me sick."

Daniel started crying. He catapulted himself into Becky's lap.

"Please, everybody. Come sit down," Becky implored, juggling the unexpected weight. "He played a trick on you. He wants you to start fighting."

"Yeh, let's not start a big hassle just because Neal is being a jerk," Nancy said with a wave of her hand, pursing her mouth into an expression of disdain.

One by one, the women shuffled away from the doors, an inch at a time, watching the others out of the corners of their eyes.

The tension lowered. Nancy, the most trusting of the four, took a step forward to return to her seat.

Suddenly, a drum burst of noise came from behind the women. The doors were vibrating like the cymbals section at an OSU football halftime. Then, a whoop went up behind them like the sound of a player who has just made the winning touchdown.

Becky turned in astonishment. Three other women also turned in astonishment. Jackie, waiting for them all to move just far away from the doors, had blasted backwards and was in the kitchen chortling out her win.

"I'm going to kill her," Maria blasted through the doors, too, fists flying.

Becky backed away. She could hear the thud of fist on flesh. She could hear the banging of bodies striking stainless steel cabinets. She could hear the pots and pans clang as they crashed to the floor.

Jackie came blasting backward through the doorway, shouting obscenities.

Daniel screamed and dug his face into her shoulder, hiding from the melee.

"Neal, make them stop." Becky's voice was pleading, desperate.

Neal was laughing uproariously. He wiped a laugh tear from his eye, and then erupted into laughter again, doubling over with the glee of it all.

"Ha. Ha. Didn't anybody ever read Irish hero tales? That's such an old trick!" Neal gloated. "Take the course. Professor Elliott teaches it. Ha, ha, ha!" He slapped his knee.

The noise of battle continued in the kitchen. Becky could hear thuds and curses and crashes.

Becky wasn't impressed with Neal's triumph. She peeled Daniel's clinging hands from her shoulders and put him down. He bounced up and down and screamed, terrified at the melee, but he could wait for a moment, Becky decided. She took a deep breath, and then went through the swinging doors. "Ladies! Ladies! Please!"

Not knowing what else to do, she inserted herself between the two of them, arms wide, shielding them from each other. She felt a kick to the shins that left her gasping in pain, but she held her ground. Maria, black hair a sweaty tangle in Becky's face, tried reaching over Becky's shoulder to punch at Jackie, but her volley was ineffective. Nancy, grateful for the respite, backed away, heading in a rush to the other side of the kitchen.

Maria was still vibrating with anger as Becky, arm in a protective shield around her shoulders, pushed her through the swinging doors and sat her down on the window seat.

Becky hovered authoritatively, pulling herself up to her full height, and willing herself into a commanding presence.

"You will not fight in my kitchen! Do you understand!" This pose worked with Daniel, Maybe it would work here.

Maria sobbed in the ebbing of her adrenalin rush. "Yes," she hissed sibilantly.

"Yes, by golly. That is my kitchen, and I demand some respect for it."

Becky felt the bowl of ice being shoved into her hand.

"Here! Put some ice on those bruises, and let's act like grownups for a change," she said, passing out the cubes to all who needed them.

She could see a new respect in Neal's eyes.

Daniel had slid down and was clinging frantically to her legs, calling "Mommy. Mommy." She picked him up again, and he jounced into his accustomed place on her hip, where he sniffled out his unhappiness.

When everyone had settled down to quiet tears or checkers again, Becky put some ice on herself. She wrapped the cubes on a towel and laid its icy chill across the vivid red at the front of her freckled shin.

"Ouch!"

That night she refused to cook.

"There's nothing left anyhow," she told Neal. "You guys had better do something about the food situation."

"Ah, come on, Becky," he whined, "Share that stock you've got hidden away upstairs."

"No way. That's for Daniel and me." Her voice was adamant.

She could hear people rustling in the kitchen, hear the slamming of cupboard doors, the banging of pots and pans.

Lee stuck her head through the swinging doors. "Come on, Becky. Work some magic with this macaroni."

What! Was she the only one with a magic wand? How difficult is it to make boxed macaroni and cheese?

In anger, she stomped upstairs, Daniel still clinging to her hip. She fed the two of them cold ravioli from a can and cut up a plateful of apple slices for dessert. The ravioli was not successful; not only did it taste strange in the mouth unheated, but it did not provide that satisfying warmth in the belly. A tear of frustration eased out of her eye.

The soft knocking at her bedroom door sounded almost decorous. She opened it with trepidation.

"Food assistance, huh?" Neal pointed at the bags lined up in the armoire. It had been hard to hide her trips up the stairway with the yellow Price Chopper bags of food.

"That's my food, Neal Hamilton. You keep your hands off."

Becky twisted inside in anguish. Hot tears rolled down her cheeks. Somehow, this was not how she had thought life would be. She remembered parties with sausages and shrimp, crackers festooned around platters of cheese, cupcakes and ice cream, a bounty spread out the length of the table. She ached to be generous, to lay out a lacy white tablecloth and invite the crowd to feast. She knew that she dared not.

"Do you get cash, too?"

"None of your business." Her voice was knife sharp.

"I don't want your food – or money either, Becky." He held his hands out, palms facing her, the ancient way of showing no weapons, an age-old human gesture of appeasement. "Actually, I was wondering if we might be able to get some food assistance, too, to help tide us over this."

Becky blinked. Of course.

Of course that was the answer. They could get some assistance, too.

"The Welfare Office is in Greenfield." Her voice became eager, volunteering information that might push then on their way. "There's a food pantry there, too."

"Greenfield? Where's that?"

"South. About 15, 20 miles."

"Twenty miles?"

Becky could see the shock in his face, and, for a moment, the absurdity of it all washed over her.

"I suppose you'd expect me to drive there, too."

"Oh, Becky, Sweetie." His voice dripped sugar, liquid and pooling in his mouth. He gave an ear-to-ear grin. "Would you?"

CHAPTER TWELVE

Parker's cabin was high on a bluff overlooking the river with a view of rolling mountain tops beyond.

"The Catskills," he told her, pointing at the purple-and-brown patterned view. "This bluff is the edge of the Poconos and that hill over there is the start of the Catskills."

Becky looked beyond to the mysterious Catskills, bemused.

"You can tell exactly where one ends and the other begins?"

"Of course. The river does it for us. Handy little thing, that river." He laughed.

She could almost hear the rolling balls of the goblins playing at bowling in the mountains beyond. She had read Washington Irving, after all.

"So that's where Rip Van Winkle fell asleep."

". . . a bit further east for that, actually – over by the Hudson. Say, how come you know so much about the legends, but so little about the countryside around here? You've lived here all your life."

"My parents were town folk. God forbid, my mother should get herself dirty tramping in the brush, and my father was always at work. I learned what I could inside four walls – from the school, from the library, from the television, and from the internet."

"How boring."

She looked down to the river below, from this height a benign slash of silver laced placidly through the bodice of the earth. She knew the peacefulness was an illusion of distance.

Daniel decided to explore the gravel of the parking area and raced away from her, bobbing from side to side as his legs pumped. She ran after him and took his hand.

"No!" He tried to pull away.

"Yes!"

She scooped him up under one arm.

"Who needs the gym?" she joked.

"Indeed," Parker seconded.

Together the two adults got the grocery bags and the diaper bag from the pickup, and carried them and a wriggling Daniel inside. Freed from her grip, the youngster ran across the room, his feet a steady patter of freedom regained. It all felt so companionable, so much like home and family. She smiled her satisfaction.

The cabin itself was very basic. One large cathedral-ceilinged room with a massive stone fireplace dominated. Behind was a small bedroom and an even smaller kitchen with a bath to the rear. Stairs led to a loft. Parker's roommate, Josh slept in the loft, he told her.

"Oh, I love it."

Parker grinned.

"National Park Service owns it. I get to live here."

She peeked in the downstairs bedroom that Parker said was his. The bed was covered with a quilt in a patchwork of brick red and ivory. A sudden vision popped into her head of herself naked and wrapped in that patchwork. Her face flamed with color. It would happen, she knew. Today? Maybe.

For now, let's concentrate on the living room, she chided herself, pulling back from the doorway.

Parker was lighting the fire, already laid in the grate.

Daniel was exploring. There, he was halfway up the stairs already.

"Come on down, young man."

Parker moved a small chest of drawers in front of the stairs to eliminate that temptation. Daniel howled his frustration, and then turned to the toy bag that Becky had carried in along with the diaper bag and Daniel's quilt.

"Here. Take your jacket off."

He held still only long enough for Becky to slide the sleeves off his arms, and then returned to his play, zooming trucks in a circle around the rag rug in front of the fireplace.

Then, Parker performed some mysterious machinations inside another cabinet and classical music flooded the cabin. Tchaikovsky. Hmm. This was a man who knew how to set an atmosphere.

"Ready to eat?"

"Umm."

Parker had Italian subs in a bag – two with ham and capicola, provolone, lettuce, tomato, and onion, oil and balsamic vinegar, and a third of plain turkey with mayonnaise.

"I am still learning what you like," he said. "The turkey is in case you don't like Italian – and for Daniel."

From another bag he revealed a two-liter bottle of Coke. Then, from some mysterious place within his refrigerator, he pulled out two cold cans of Budweiser. The small, round table was set for three, with paper plates and red-checked paper napkins.

Becky popped the top on her Budweiser and smiled. She could get to like this – get to like this very much indeed.

Parker sat down across from her, and Daniel grabbed onto his leg, trying to climb onto his lap. Parker gave a boost and soon the three of them were seated at the table, Daniel stuffing bite-size bits of turkey and bread into his mouth s fast as he could.

"Chew!" she reminded him. "Then, swallow!"

She munched on her sub, tasting the tartness of the cheese and the salty smoothness of the ham, the sourness of the vinegar, and the sweetness of the bread, relishing the cold tang of onion and the bursts of heat of the black pepper grains, sure that she had arrived at Valhalla.

After lunch, Daniel fell asleep on Parker's bed, tucked underneath his own Thomas the Tank Engine blanket. Becky was always glad for this afternoon respite, a few moments for herself.

Today, the time would be for herself and Parker.

He put another log on the fire and joined her on the couch.

"I brought you up here so we could talk alone, Becky."

Her face grinned ear to ear at the concept.

"How are you doing with your busload of hippies?"

Her face collapsed at the thought of them; her shoulders turned down.

"Not good, heh?" He commiserated with her.

"Well, I suppose it's okay. They are trying to help out, to not be too much of a bother, but I really want them on their way."

"The problem is, even if they leave, then you'd be down there alone, and winter is coming on. You could move out. Haven't you got anywhere else to go?"

"No, not really."

"You know, you are setting yourself up to be a victim in all this." His voice was tart. "I do not like seeing you as the victim."

"What do you mean?"

"I mean your powerlessness in this whole thing – in being alone, in being a single mother, in having no education, in having no money, in having no resources, in having no choice."

He struck his knee with his hand with each point.

"People who are powerless are always the ones who are victimized."

She stared at him in exasperation. Her secret grievances against life, the yawning chasm of inadequacy that had opened up inside her in the past few weeks, the sudden and unexpected flood of desire for the university experience the group members were throwing away were not supposed to be so – so – public. Even for somebody like Parker. She sat up straight in indignation.

"Am I supposed to be offended here? I thought you liked me the way I am!"

"No, don't be offended. I'm saying this because I do like you. I like you for yourself – but not for your situation, not for your power-lessness. Come on, Becky. Wake up. Figure out how to give yourself a choice in life. You can do better than this."

Her mouth fell open.

"I like you a whole lot, as a matter of fact."

In his agitation, he jumped up and began to pace the room.

"One example – your parents? Can't your parents give you some help? Life for you would be a heck of a lot easier if you could get some help from that direction."

Tears welled up in her eyes, and her voice caught in her throat as she spoke. "Dan is a year-and-a-half year old. They haven't given me any help in all that time. I haven't even seen them or heard from them."

"Would you accept it if they offered?"

Becky's insides melted like Jell-O on top of a woodstove.

"Oh, yes," she whimpered. "I would. I would not at first, because they treated me so badly, but now I know how hard it all is."

She blew her nose in her napkin.

"Besides," she went on breathlessly. "I want them to love me. Why don't they love me?"

Her sobs rose into the high-pitched wail of hysteria of the aban-doned child.

Parker took her in his arms, laying her head on his shoulder, comforting her.

"Shh. Shh. You'll wake Daniel."

Her crying diminished, and he handed her another napkin to replace the one soggy and crumpled in her fist.

"From what you have described, Becky, your parents were in shock when you got pregnant. They've had plenty of time to get over that, and, besides, one thing about grandparents – put the baby in their laps, and they fall in love; all is then forgiven. Have you even tried to take Daniel to see them?"

"No."

"Why don't you?"

She sobbed. "I'm afraid. They always make me feel so – so wrong. I did not want to feel wrong. I wanted to love my baby. I wanted to be a good mother." She hiccupped. "Daniel is not wrong. He is so very right. He is my treasure."

"Why don't you give them a chance to see how very right he is?"

"I'm afraid." She wailed her anguish into the disintegrating napkin.

"Do you want me to talk to them?"

Becky blinked, and then opened a long gaze through her tear-stained lashes. This was a different emotion rising up in her breast, and she took a moment to sort it out, hiccuping softly while she thought.

Carefully, walking gingerly on the stepping stones of their growing relationship, she asked, "Would you do this in an official capacity, or because you are my friend?"

He understood. His voice went low and soft. "I would do this because I care for you."

"Do you care?"

"Yes."

"I need somebody to care." A tear dripped off her eyelash. She dabbed at it with the napkin.

"I know you do." He paused staring out the window at the blue infinity of the sky beyond. Then, he took up his courage and said, "I need somebody to care, too."

The sudden updraft of this new idea sent Becky's heart spinning wildly on its axis. She had been afraid to care, afraid she would get hurt like she had been so many times in the past. He was inviting her in, chiding her that she had not taken the bridge across that brook yet, but she was still not sure she could open up in that way to Parker.

"I can see how much you love Daniel; I know that you can love," he said softly, "so I will be patient. But I also know there is too much weight on you right now. Let's try to get some of it off. I'll talk to your parents – and we have to get these people on their way, too."

"No, Parker. I'll talk to them. I'll do it." She was struck by the rightness of it all. "My parents are my responsibility, and I have to do it myself."

Suddenly, she was sobbing again, and Parker's arms were around her, gently holding, comforting. There were no demands as he held her in the lengthening shadows of afternoon.

CHAPTER THIRTEEN

"**M**ary Ellen and Susan have appointments with the orthopedist. Could you drive us into town?"

Funny thing – She did not recall opening a free taxi service. Becky counted to ten, stifling a slow burn all the while.

"I'll go grocery shopping at the same time."

Neal knew how to get to a girl.

"Sure," she said between clenched teeth.

Together they bundled Mary Ellen and Susan, proud possessors of the worst broken bones and the biggest casts – and Daniel in his car seat – into the old blue sedan. Neal, scrunched sideways trying to fit as the third in the middle of the back seat, looked like a discarded scarecrow tossed aside at the end of the season.

"I guess we can put the groceries in the trunk," he wheezed.

"Umm, yes."

"Don't you gals have parents who can help?" Becky listened to herself as if from far away, as she turned the key in the ignition. She had parents on her mind. Even as she asked, Becky felt her own guilt rise up to choke her.

"Sure, but they're in Ohio. My doctor is here," Mary Ellen said with a poker face.

"Aren't there any doctors in Ohio?"

"Of course. Duh! But my insurance demands that I get follow-up care from the same doctor who treated me in the first place. The follow-up care is all included in the initial bill – one price covers all – and they won't pay it twice."

"Me, too," Susan echoed.

"What about the accident policy on the bus?"

A silence hung in the car.

"Humph. Not sure he has an accident policy."

"Oh."

Another long silence hung, punctuated only by the sound of the tires humming on macadam.

". . . doesn't make sense that you can't go home." Becky felt her face burn. ". . . doesn't make sense at all."

The cloud of guilt hovered as she pulled into the parking lot of the doctor's office, nagged at her as she and Neal helped the two women into the waiting room, became a steady throbbing behind her temples as she dropped Neal off at the Price Chopper.

"You're not coming in?" he asked, tilting his head in an expression of surprise.

"No, I have an errand. I'll pick you up in an hour or so."

She waved her hand dismissing the importance of this errand, but her brow furrowed into lines of worry. She drove the State Bank block without thinking. She passed the town library block in a fog of uncertainty. She made the turn by the Dingle Dairy Store wavering in her determination. She only progressed along Baker's Farm Road, heading into a residential subdivision, because for the first quarter mile there was no place to turn around. Then, it was too late. She had come to the big colonial nestled behind a row of spruce trees, paved driveway giving access off Baker's Farm Road. Prickles ran up and down the back of her neck. She did not have to stop. She could just keep going, do a drive-by, run and hide, but somehow her battered blue car was in the driveway.

How did it get in the driveway?

The frost cracked cold underfoot as Becky stepped out of her car onto the pavement. For a brief moment she stood there assessing her errand, a fool's errand she was sure. She felt a tickle of anxiety ooze down her lumbar column a disc at a time, playing a maddening melody of inadequacy.

What if she's not home?

Oh, don't be silly. What difference would it make? She'd just be alone again, alone as she had been all along, alone and safe from disapproving eyes and malice-tart tongues.

What if she turns you away?

Becky knew that she was getting cold feet. She slammed the car door, announcing her arrival in no uncertain terms. Let whoever wished come forth to greet her. This was a dual undertaking, after all. She did not have to walk alone on those last 10 feet up the long, long sidewalk, climb those two brick steps leading to the frightening heights.

Then, as Becky reached into the back seat for Daniel, unhooking him from the car seat, her mother, Sabrina, appeared in the doorway looking very much as Becky had remembered her.

Is that a smile? Or a frown? Open the storm door. I want to see, Becky thought. Yes, a smile. A bit tentative, perhaps, but a smile. I am welcome.

They hugged. Across the haze of those last 10 feet, across light years of non-understanding, they hugged.

"Mom, I want you to meet Daniel." Becky choked over the words. She pulled his hand from his mouth and wiped at the teething slobber with a tissue. She wanted him to look like a gentleman in the making.

"I'm so glad. Let me see. Let me see." Tears began to streak her carefully applied makeup. "Oh, how beautiful. Come in, come in. I want to see."

Inside the house, Becky, breathless, silent, pulled off Daniel's hood and unzipped his jacket.

"Oh, auburn hair. Oh, look at those eyes. Oh, how beautiful." The tears poured down Sabrina's face.

"Daniel, meet your Grandma," Becky said.

"Grandma Jane?" he said loud and clear, suddenly aroused to a language capability he'd never displayed before.

Becky colored.

"No. Grandma Sabrina." Turning to her mother, in befuddlement and tripping over her words, she asked, "Is that what you want to be called?"

"Grandma Sabrina is just fine. He can call me Grandma Sabrina. I hate that Nana thing, it sounds like a servant to me, and Granny is almost worse." She gave a motion of distaste, over the thought of Granny living in the backwoods. "Grandma Sabrina is a good choice."

After a pause, she queried, "I guess the Wilsons see a lot of him."

Becky sighed.

". . . one weekend a month."

"I hope they are helping you with child support."

"Yes."

Silence fell for a moment. Daniel squirmed off Becky's lap.

"I suppose we should have done that, too."

Becky bit her lip.

Daniel began to explore, running off on still-fat toddler legs,

Becky, awkward, mindful of the knickknacks, mindful of the lamps, ran after him and corralled him in the dining room. He laughed in his freedom, and she laughed in response. Then, she picked him up in her arms and returned to the living room. She paused in the archway, unsure, aware that her mother was looking at her, piercing blue eyes scanning for imperfections. Was her hair combed? Was Daniel's sweatshirt clean?

"You look so happy with him," Sabrina said softly.

"I am so happy. He is my treasure."

"I can see that."

A long silence fell as Becky came back into the room carrying Daniel. He squirmed to be put down.

"Oh, let him run a bit," said Sabrina.

She picked up the flower arrangement from the coffee table and put it on top of the china cabinet.

"I guess I should child-proof this house. I've been meaning to do that." She picked up the vanilla candles, which seemed headed for the same high spot.

"Are you still living with Mac MacGreavey?"

"Umm, no. Actually, we broke up." A red stain crept up Becky's neck and spread to her cheeks, flushing her face with embarrassment.

"Oh." Sabrina's eyebrows lifted in surprise. "Good. We never did approve of Mac MacGreavey."

How ever did she know about Mac MacGreavey?

Becky's throat tightened. She opened her hands in a gesture of helplessness.

"So where are you living now?"

"At the Duck Point Inn -- you know, that old place on the River Road north of town. I am the caretaker." Becky emphasized the word caretaker, hoping that the responsibility of a caretaker's job would add its cachet to this conversation.

It certainly did. Her mother's face brightened. "A caretaker? You have a job?"

"Yes." Becky felt a pang of guilt at describing her residence at the Duck Point Inn as a job. She could not overcome the feeling that there was some underlying rationale at work in the situation of the inn that she did not understand. Yet, she acknowledged to herself, she had been industrious in her raking of leaves, in her re-nailing of dangling shingles, in her scraping of grease off the kitchen floor. Lou was getting value from her work. With a roof over her head and a comfortable bed, she was getting value in her turn. With a tamping down of her overwrought conscience, she decided that this exchange of value could qualify as a job.

"Do you have a boyfriend?"

"Umm, yes." Oh, back to that old sticky subject. Becky did not want to say too much here.

"Cookie." Daniel interrupted, clinging to Becky's legs. "Cookie." His talking was suddenly very purposeful.

"I don't have any cookies, I'm sorry." Sabrina wrinkled her nose in dismay. "But would you like some lunch?"

"I can't stay today, Mom. I have people waiting for me to pick them up. I just wanted to stop by and say hello."

"Oh, I'm sorry." Sabrina looked crestfallen. "But you'll come back. Oh, please tell me you'll come back."

"Yes, we'll come back." Becky let out a long-held breath. She was exceedingly glad about being invited back.

"Thanksgiving. Come for Thanksgiving, please!"

Becky paused, uncertain about the formality of Thanksgiving, with china and linen and candles, hardly the place for Daniel and his shenanigans. Then, she saw the eagerness in her mother's face and felt something hard and cold release inside herself, a catch to a long disused and hidden lockbox.

". . . and bring your young man." Sabrina smiled.

"Yes, Thanksgiving," Becky whispered through a dry throat. "We'll come. I'll ask Parker."

"Your father will be so happy."

I hope so, Becky concluded, as she zipped Daniel's jacket to leave. I hope so.

Later, Becky arrived back at the inn with her load of passengers and groceries to find that Lou, the phantom landlord, had come and gone, turning off the water and draining the pipes.

"He said it was necessary," explained Cliff with a shrug of his shoulders. "He said we could stay so long as we were willing to cope."

"Yes, necessary," seconded Becky with a sigh. But this truly put the inn into winter mode. She wondered how they were going to survive. Willing was one thing; actuality was another.

Meals at the inn became an array of sandwiches or nourishment out of cans, anything to avoid the necessity of washing dishes, and the inn-habitants all learned the function of the old-fashioned chamber pots beneath their beds as the nighttime temperatures dropped low and lower.

CHAPTER FOURTEEN

"Hey, Becky."

The shout resounded up the stairway and echoed down the hallway.

What do those guys want now? Becky rolled her eyes.

"You've got a visitor!"

Huh?

She dropped her magazine, the recipe for easy-to-cook Southwest Chicken abandoned in favor of this brand-new concept. A visitor!

Parker? No, not Parker!

"Daddy!"

Her father, Andrew Rowe, stood there looking up at her. He was tanned from many summer days spent on the golf course, and the freckles across his face merged into a pleasing mélange of color. His maroon polyester slacks with tight-pressed creases, gray golfing sweater with maroon preppie stripe, gray golfing shoes, white hair neatly combed over the balding spot made a silhouette of business and social conservatism in the midst of the patchwork disorder below.

The Phishermen, for once, were silent. Not a sound emerged from any of them. Not one movement split the tableau of the moment. They, too, were staring at this apparition, aware that something momentous was taking place.

Becky took the scene in all in one excruciating moment. She saw the expectant faces looking up at her, mouths open in commiseration.

She saw the white casts tilted at one angle, and crutches at another. She saw the broad array of grimy quilts mingled with discarded dishes waiting to be gathered and washed. Most of all, she was aware of the haze of blue smoke hanging in waves in the high vee of the open-raftered ceiling, of the cloying, sweet smell of it all.

"Come up," she stammered. "Come up."

At the top of the stairs, he hugged her. She shivered in his arms and felt a tear rise in her eye.

"It's so good to see you."

"Come in. Come in."

Oh, can't I just say something sensible, she thought.

"I was just on my way to a golf game, and I thought I'd stop in and say hello."

"They're still playing in this cold?"

"Sure! We play faster, that's all – no dawdling -- so we can get back to the clubhouse." His laugh was deep, a welcome bass note in the room.

The room was warm with the morning sun pouring in the window. Daniel was in the midst of a nap, sleeping with his legs tucked underneath him and his white-diapered rump in the air. He had thrown off his Thomas the Tank Engine blanket, and his chubby legs were bare.

"Daniel. Did you say his name is Daniel?" he whispered.

"Yes."

"Facing lions in the den?"

"Lions?"

"That crew downstairs – Daniel in the lion's den."

"Oh." She had known he'd get around to that.

"I hope you're not smoking that stuff."

"Oh, no. Not me." Her face fell.

"I'm sorry," he apologized. "I didn't come here to chide you."

"It's okay, Dad. I try to stay up here away from it with Daniel."

She offered him the rocking chair and perched herself on the bed.

For a moment, he rocked companionably. Becky felt the delirious smile rise again; the force of it hurt her cheeks.

"I came because I wanted to meet Daniel and to see you. I missed you the other day when you visited your mother."

Becky nodded.

"I'm glad you came around," he continued. ". . . really glad."

Silence fell over the bedroom, broken only by Daniel's snuffling. Becky didn't know what to say.

"She said you're coming for Thanksgiving. Good! Good!"

Andrew rubbed his hands back and forth. Was it satisfaction, Becky wondered, or was he warming himself?

Seeing her look, he commented, "Itchy palms."

"They say that means you're going to get money." She smiled.

Oh, how stupid, she thought. An aphorism! There must be something intelligent to talk about. Her anxiety tickled her diaphragm.

"That would be nice." He, too, smiled.

Well, at least they were smiling at each other.

Daniel woke up and sat up in the crib, the side of his face red and lined from lying on the wrinkled sheet. He rubbed his eyes, stretched, and stood up, leaning against the side of the crib, arms reaching for Becky.

"Out! Out!"

Becky picked him up. He clung to her as he sat on her hip. He smelled of sweat and urine.

"Dannie, say hello to your Grandpa."

He was shy, though, and tucked his head into her shoulder, looking at the stranger in his bedroom out of the corner of one eye.

"Hello, Daniel. I'm glad to meet you. I hope we'll be good friends."

He patted the boy's back tentatively. Daniel peeked out from the shoulder hiding place, a smile turning up the corner of his mouth. Then, he huddled back into Becky's chest, and hunched his shoulders.

"He'll get used to you. He's just being shy."

"I know he will. I hope we have a lot of good times together. You know, I always wanted a son."

Becky's face fell again. Her shoulders slumped.

"I mean, not to replace you." He spoke quickly, and his eyes swiveled upward. "I'm sorry again; I'm putting my foot in my mouth today. I meant another child. I would have liked another child – one of each – girl – boy."

He hugged the two of them, his big arms circling her with Daniel between them. Daniel squirmed in the squishing of the hug.

"Now I've got two, and I love you both."

Becky bit her lips.

"I love you, too, Dad."

"I want to be a grandpa to this kid."

"Good."

"I want to be a father to you, too. I should have come around long before this. I don't know what I was thinking."

"I didn't come around either," she said. "I was wrong. I'm sorry."

"So how do we start?"

"I guess we just start like this. This kid smells like he needs to be changed. Want to stick around for that."

Andrew smiled. "Sure. Why not? I have to admit, that is not my department, though. I've never changed a diaper in my life."

". . . too busy bringing home the bacon, heh?" Becky grinned.

"Yep." He grimaced wanly in response, and threw his hands apart, apologizing for his inadequacies. "The bills keep coming. Your mother spends; I try to pay for it all."

"Daniel, Daniel. Loosen your grip. Let go. It's time to get changed."

The squeak of the rocker on the wood floor punctuated the silence as Becky cleaned up Daniel and taped a new diaper in place. Daniel was busy all the while trying to see this new person in his life, chuckling his toddler laugh, assessing.

Becky added a clean, long-sleeved shirt, a pair of corduroy bib overalls, and shoes and socks to the squirming bit of boy in the crib. Then, giving a brush to his hair, she picked him up. This time he held his arms out for his grandpa, and Becky handed him over. She sat back on the bed comfortable to watch the two as they jabbered at each other and got acquainted. Her smile seemed to go on forever.

CHAPTER FIFTEEN

Daniel was asleep, finally. "Itsy, Bitsy Spider" had gone on much too long, and Becky was tired. She was also perturbed. After he drifted off, she folded herself into a quilt and blew out the candle. Moonlight shone in through the 12-paned window, and she could see the outlines of the room, a sheltering enclosure beyond which dragons and other monsters of the night roamed. These mythical creatures were nothing compared to the real-life perplexities she had to deal with. She propped up the pillows behind her back and assumed a thinking position. She brushed her hand through her hair, took a deep, oxygenating breath, and settled in for a good think. This situation could not go on.

What were her alternatives?

She could leave, which would be the perfect answer if she had anyplace else to go. Certainly, she'd done it before. But, by golly, she was here first. They had moved in on her. Territorialism was a powerful motivator, she realized.

. . . and besides, it was November. Who wanted to camp out in this kind of weather? Going back to living in the car was just not an option.

On the other hand, she could convince Neal to stop abusing her good nature. What was it the advice columnists always said? You can't be abused unless you let yourself be abused. Maybe having a compliant nature was not the most desirable thing in the present situation.

Leaving a bad situation had always been the easy alternative, she realized. By simply leaving, she did not have to assert herself.

Somehow, she determined, somehow she was going to have to find it in herself to stand up to Neal and his many demands.

She reached deep inside herself to find that place of strength, building a fortification in her psyche brick by brick.

Thanksgiving was coming up, and Becky knew she had to get clean before the big feast. The day was going to be too important to show up unshowered and grimy with wood ash.

Also, it had gotten too cold to do any wash by hand, and the piles of dirty clothes and bedding were getting larger. Becky collected everything, making sure to check under the bed and in the cracks and crevices for any stray socks or shirts. She trekked down the stairs with the black plastic bags of dirty wash first, while Daniel, dressed in his last clean outfit, rolled around in his crib exploring the red laces of his sneakers. Two trips later, she retied the laces, added his jacket and hat, and picked him up.

Neal was standing at the foot of the stairs, blocking her way. "Heading out?"

"Yes."

"How about a ride to town?"

"Not today." Firm, firm, she cautioned herself. Calm and firm.

"You're going to the laundromat. We sure could use a trip to the laundromat."

All conversation in the dining room had stopped, and all the faces were turned toward the confrontation on the stairs. Lee paused in the middle of spooning something from a bowl into her mouth. What was it she had? Where did they find food? Becky hoped Lee hadn't stolen it from her hidden supply.

"Do you have any money for the Laundromat?"

"No, but you do!"

"I don't think so. Actually, I have other plans for today, and I have other plans for my money. Excuse me, please."

He didn't respond.

"Move!" Her voice was cold. She stared him in the eye, practicing her new-found determination.

He half moved, shuffling slightly away so she could squeeze past his bulk. Daniel kicked out as they brushed past and hit Neal on his sweatshirt-cushioned arm. For once, Becky did not chide her son for rudeness.

Neal coughed slightly and turned into the dining room, shrugging as he approached the others. The group began to shift and squirm again, conversations resuming. Lee tipped the bowl up to spoon out the last few curds of whatever it was – Oatmeal? Applesauce?

Becky headed straight for the door, opened it, and walked out briskly before anybody had a chance to crank up the whining. Holding her breath, she buckled Daniel into his car seat, climbed into the driver's seat, and turned the key in the ignition. She was heading up the driveway slope, icy gravel crunching underneath her tires, before she breathed the first sigh of relief. One battle had been won. Her heart was pounding in her chest, and she breathed slowly and steadily to calm herself. She vowed to analyze this success so she could do it again, but not right this minute. First she had to get all these fluttery parts of herself, her traumatized brain and her upside-down stomach and her quivery arms, in working order so she could get on with her busy day.

At the Greenfield High School pool, Becky heard the swimmers before she saw them. As she opened the entry door to the swimming pool annex, the high-pitched voices of children and parents sounded, echoing in odd geometrics around the octagonal dome.

The dome was steamy and smelled of chlorine. Streams of sunlight played pick-up sticks in the arch of the dome and settled into a tropical haze above the pool. Reflections from the water played across the aqua-painted walls and cast waves of light and shadow back to the reinforced glass triangles of the roof. Becky felt like she was underwater.

Family swim was held every Saturday from 1 to 3 p.m. She did not always want to spend the money, but today was different. Today she was getting rid of the blood, sweat, and tears and making herself over into the lovely young woman, the socially acceptable person her mother and father wanted her to be. She would start with cleanliness.

She paused at the registration table, and pulled out her wallet.

"Three fifty," the kid in red beach shorts announced. ". . . and swim diapers are required for all children under the age of three."

She'd flirt with him, but he looked too into himself with those six-pack abs, and the carefully arranged hair. Becky dismissed the thought in a hurry.

She handed him four singles and got back two quarters.

"Is the water warm?"

"Well, sort of."

That meant it was darn cold, Becky decided. She gritted her teeth. If the swim was short – even if the swim was non-existent – that would be okay. What she really wanted was the hot showers in the locker room.

In the meantime, though, several families were already playing in the pool, parents standing up to their waists in the shallow end supporting little kids who flailed and kicked, while older kids pretended they were dolphins leaping and diving through the water. A couple of young teens were even swimming laps, applying an earnestness of purpose that surely would get them somewhere someday. The pool scene looked like it had potential – nobody had turned into an icicle – so Becky decided to give it a try.

In the locker room, she changed herself and Daniel into bathing suits. He also wore the required swim diaper and an inflatable swim vest, making him a roly-poly toy version of himself.

Becky had struggled over the purchase of those swim diapers. Should she spend the money or not? One package of swim diapers could last her the whole winter, she reasoned. She'd use them one a week, and that would enable this hot and steamy break every Saturday.

Becky slipped into her flip-flops, locked the gym bag, the diaper bag, their clothes, their coats, and her purse into a locker, put the lanyard with the key around her neck, and picked up Daniel, who was slippery in her arms, an unfamiliar load with all his swim gear in place. Nothing worthwhile is simple, she reminded herself. She pursed her lips and wrinkled her nose. Then, taking a deep breath, she headed through the doorway to the pool.

Stepping down into the water, she grimaced. It was freezing.

Another mom standing just below her noticed her hesitation.

"Come on in," she said, "It's not so bad once you get used to it."

"This pool always used to be so warm," Becky said. "What happened?"

"I think they turned the heat down to save money."

"I see. Everybody's into saving money."

"The whole world is afflicted with that problem."

Daniel was clinging to her neck, already shivering.

"It's okay, Daniel. It's okay."

She splashed him a little bit at a time so he would get used to the water. Then, he reached down, trying to grab the water himself. She lowered the two of them another step into the depths. Finally, one step at a time, they got wet.

Becky couldn't do much swimming with Daniel clinging to her like a limpet, but they bounced up and down for a while, talking now and then to the other parents in the pool, playing hide-and-seek with a toddler girl with dark hair plastered in wet streaks across her forehead.

Then, hypothermia began to creep up on Becky. Enough of this cold soak, she thought; her fingers were turning blue. She climbed out, wrapped a towel around Daniel, jumped up and down a bit to start the blood flowing, and headed for the showers.

Hot! And clean! Shampoo bubbles flowed down her back. What could be better?

Daniel was already scrubbed. He sat on a clean towel in the locker room and built a plastic block tower while Becky showered. The curtain was open so she could keep an eye on him. No privacy, she complained to herself – no privacy for a mother. She even had to jump out once, nude and soapy, when he lost attention in the blocks and pushed himself to his feet ready to run. "Oh, no. Don't run in here. The tiles are wet and slippery."

She half-wrapped a towel around herself as she chased him. Fortunately, the locker room was empty of spectators to this folly.

"Please learn to walk," Becky suggested. "Run is not the only mode of locomotion."

Even in her arms, wrapped in a towel, his legs continued to pump. Up, down, bend and bounce, he was going somewhere. He squealed his delight.

Becky wasn't sure which one of them was going to win this marathon of childhood, but, at least, for one day – for the all-important Thanksgiving visit ahead – they would be clean.

CHAPTER SIXTEEN

Entering her parents' house for Thanksgiving brought a chill to Becky's body. Her shoulders hunched over, and she shivered uncontrollably in anticipation. Her father, though, was waiting with a hug. She was barely inside the door before she was enveloped in his sweater-clad arms; she could smell the cedar closet. Daniel squirmed in the midst of the bear hug.

"Dad, I want you to meet my friend, Parker Sims. Parker, this is Dad – Andrew Rowe. He works at the Pennsylvania Commonwealth Bank. Parker's a National Park ranger, Dad."

Andrew shook Parker's hand, pumping it with a convivial welcome. Becky recognized the social pattern. We can do business, he was saying as he invited him in -- never mind that the business in this case was over daughter and grandson.

He hung their coats in the entryway closet, a welcoming ritual that Becky barely noticed, because her mother appeared carrying a huge, gift-wrapped package.

"Here's a little something for Daniel."

Becky was flustered. "I didn't know it was Christmas."

"No. We're just head over heels into being grandparents. It was my first chance to shop in the children's department, and I enjoyed it thoroughly."

"Sabrina, meet Parker." Andrew continued the introductions with a hearty demeanor. He smiled broadly being an eager host.

In the living room, Becky sat close to the wood fire. She could smell the turkey cooking in the oven. Her hunger came alive, and she swallowed hard. Dinner wasn't ready yet. Patience. Patience.

Daniel was placed in front of the gaily-festooned package. He loved the bow, but he wasn't quite sure what to do with the rest of it, so Becky helped him tear off the paper and open the box.

"Look," she cooed. "Clothes."

Daniel knew exactly what to do with the newsboy-style tweed cap, the first thing revealed from the tissue paper. He plopped it on his head with the aplomb of a fashion-plate adolescent.

Sabrina clapped. Her joy was transparent. Maybe this might work after all, Becky thought, and then chided herself for being so greedy over a present.

Bringing herself back to the moment, Becky explored the box, finding an outfit of warm cocoa brown corduroy pants, an ivory plaid shirt with a collar, and a warm cocoa brown cardigan sweater with little leather patches on the elbows.

"How adorable!"

Sabrina glowed with happiness.

"I've never had a little boy to shop for before. It was great fun."

Becky felt the smile expand from the center of her face into a Cheshire cat grin that tested the limits of her cheeks.

"This outfit is absolutely marvelous. Thank you."

Becky knew they'd want to see him in the new outfit. Daniel was soon upended, his too-big denims exchanged for the soft-wale corduroys. After he was dressed again, Becky stowed the old set of clothes in his diaper bag. He did look marvelous, a miniature version of an English country gentleman.

She plastered the orange bow on her own sweater, though. Suddenly she felt festive. It was a day for gladness and joy, after all, a day for giving a multitude of thanks.

Daniel gave his thanks by running from the living room into the dining room. His new sneakers pattered on the oak floor and were muffled by the rug. He listened carefully to the change in sound. Then, finding a strange dining room a bit too much adventure for one little boy, he pattered back to Becky and climbed onto her lap. He was getting much steadier on his feet, Becky noticed. Such expeditions were taken with a growing sense of confidence

Dinner finally was served. From the shrimp cocktail appetizer to the pumpkin pie dessert, the feast was a delight for Becky's taste buds. She took deep bites of the turkey breast enjoying the rich taste of the meat. She rolled the mashed potatoes around in her mouth savoring the buttery carbohydrate goodness. She bit into the broccoli with cheese sauce and crunched on the fresh green salad, sure that she had gone to a gastronomic heaven.

"Becky always was a good eater." Her father's voice, holiday hearty, boomed across the table, addressing everyone, addressing no one.

Becky cringed at being recalled as a child, a good eater. Daniel was the good eater now. Then, her mother told a tale about that purple hair Becky had sported for a junior high school dance. Their recollections were all of a childhood that Becky had tucked away with her dolls. Could they not have some sense of her as a grownup woman? Had she not matured in all that time?

Her face burned. She quenched the fire inside with another glass of Coke, frosty with ice cubes.

"The visit might be painful," she had warned Parker, inviting him to accompany her to this food-oriented reunion, hoping she'd feel better with him on her side. Now, though, she was embarrassed.

"I don't feel at all like that child they are remembering," she told him over coffee.

"But that was their child!" Parker's face split into a devilish grin. "You were their child – their only child -- and everything you did was just marvelous – just the way Daniel is marvelous to you now."

She smiled broadly. Marvelous Daniel was a subject after her own heart.

Naptime for Daniel brought another round of déjà vu.

Becky lay on the bed with him briefly, waiting for him to settle down to sleep in this strange room. She was fighting the post-turkey lethargy by contemplating the sun's glare through the lacy white curtains and counting the blossoms in the pink-flowered wallpaper of her childhood bedroom. Some things never change, and this room, with its maple dressers and pressed-flower pictures, was one of them.

Sabrina had decorated this room in appropriate little-girl-child style. Becky had never been allowed to put up posters or add the gee-gaws that would have made it her own. She had never been allowed to tear apart the closet looking for just the right outfit or disturb the pristine arrangement of the dresser drawers. Becky felt curiously disconnected from the years she had spent living in this room.

Becky sighed.

Later, the two men went to look at the model trains and busses displayed as a very expensive collection on the white-painted book shelves of the home office while the two women went to the kitchen – Sabrina's kitchen – to clean up the cooking debris and wash the very expensive china and glassware.

"Are you serious about this young man?"

Becky had thought that her mother would ask this question. It, along with the turkey and pumpkin pie, were the inevitables of the day.

The moment was awkward, though. Becky, embarrassed at being asked, hovered over the Lenox china she was soaping with a yellow sponge. Sabrina seemed equally embarrassed at the asking; she was busy contemplating the interior of the side-by-side refrigerator. Both knew it was a subject burning in Sabrina's psyche – the social conventions were important to her -- and this was a question that must be answered.

"I've only know him a few weeks," Becky apologized, "but we get along really well. I like him a whole lot, but it's just too soon to tell how serious it is."

"What does he do?" Of course Sabrina would ask this question.

"He's a National Park ranger."

"I don't think I've ever known a National Park ranger before. Is that a job that could support a home and family?"

Becky hesitated, picking her way carefully through this minefield.

"It's a federal job, Mom. . . . with all the federal benefits. It's a very good, professional job. He deals with the outdoors and recreation, but those need good men, too."

Sabrina seemed satisfied with that, content that her overly eager daughter who had galloped headlong into motherhood, burning her bridges behind her, was displaying some sense at last.

The exchange opened up a vortex of yearning inside Becky. Just how serious was this relationship with Parker? As a matter of fact, just how keen was she in living in the back country of Yellowstone National Park? Her brow furrowed, and her mouth crinkled as she contemplated these question and their possible answers.

Sabrina wanted a neat package, all tied up with a pretty bow, just like that pretty package she had given Daniel. A stable marriage to a competent, conservative breadwinner suited Sabrina. This tastefully decorated house suited her. Becky, on the other hand, had been content to walk along through the new relationship with Parker, enjoying its growth, and not wondering where it was going.

But now she wondered.

She was angry at Sabrina for making her wonder, for making her yearn for more than she already had, for confusing her as to what she really wanted.

Mom, stop layering your values over me; I don't need a template, Becky thought. But the desire stuck in her throat, and she could not deny it.

Before the day was over, her parents – surprisingly – had offered some babysitting. Becky had the feeling that, despite Sabrina's chanting of grandmotherly platitudes, her mother was doing charity work when she offered. Sabrina would put babysitting Daniel on the calendar along with the Ladies' Guild and volunteering at the hospital.

Becky would take the help, though. She would take it for now, she knew. That was why she was here, watching a late-afternoon video on her father's very expensive, LED, 54-inch, wall-mounted television, while sitting next to Parker on the very expensive brocade sofa. She lost track of the plot, though, because she was busy shifting those templates in her head.

This yearning for Parker? That was a completely different feeling than she'd ever experienced. There was no template laid on her here. She knew that this yearning for the man sitting beside her, arm around her shoulders as they watched television, smelling of aftershave and the woods, had nothing to do with Sabrina's ordered life, but was something untamed and disordered, something prehistoric surging up from an unexplored wilderness deep inside herself.

CHAPTER SEVENTEEN

"**W**hat would you like to be doing?"

"Doing?" Becky asked, puzzled by the notion.

"You know – doing! I mean, if you weren't here cooking dinner for a bunch of potheads. I mean, if you weren't a mom and taking care of Daniel. What would be your choice if you had all the choice in the world?" Jackie's conversation starter was provocative.

Becky scowled. It wasn't a question she really wanted to contemplate.

"I mean really!"

Jackie, up to her elbows at the sink, inched her sweatshirt sleeves a little higher, and rolled the soapy sponge over a crackled white stoneware plate. The bulk of Maria loomed beyond, a silent figure drying and putting the dishes away. The two women had made up quickly after the fight and were friends again.

"Where would you want to be? What would you want to be doing? What would your choices be?"

"I haven't got any choices. I've got to take care of Daniel."

". . . but if you did?"

Becky moved the broom a little harder, pretending she was really interested in the dust in the corners of the kitchen. Daniel pulled at her denim-covered leg, demanding her attention. Then he sat down, scattering the pile of swept-up dirt back into the corners. Becky picked him up and sat him down again away from the area being swept.

"Stay there!" Her voice was firm.

"Well?" Jackie wouldn't let it go.

"I think I'd be curled up somewhere warm reading a good book."

"You like to read?"

"Yes, and I don't get much chance to do it with Daniel so active. I have to keep an eye on him all the time."

"I can see that. He's a ball of fire, for sure, and you don't get much rest, but I think that's just interfering with the basic level of your desires."

Daniel rolled over and drummed his feet on the floor --- one, two, one, two. The sound of his sneakers hitting the tiles echoed in the cavernous kitchen. He giggled at the noise. He was making it; he also was making it stop. For a moment he was lying in one place, contemplating the process and his role in it. Becky did not have to run after him.

". . . the basic level? What do you mean?"

"I mean that is just the most essential of your desires. You need some quiet time for yourself. If I had asked you the same question before dinner you might have answered 'spaghetti and meatballs' because you were hungry."

"I see."

"That's right in front of you -- but I mean, what are your deepest desires – the ones that would bring you to self-actualization."

". . . self-actualization?" The concept was brand-new to Becky.

"I see you really haven't given any thought to it. According to the psychologists, there are several levels of needs. First, there are those physiological ones; we have to eat and sleep and breathe. Next we have safety needs, followed by social needs. Then we have the self-esteem needs of a person. I think you are filling a lot of self-esteem needs by trying to be a good mother."

"Oh, really." Becky's voice was dry. This suddenly sounded like a textbook.

"Yes, and you are doing a good job of it, too."

"Thanks."

". . . but I think you are bending over backwards trying to be a good mother because your own mother left a void to be filled."

Becky's cheeks flushed. She didn't know what to say. She coughed.

"I guess you've had psychology courses at the university."

"Nah. I learned that in my public-speaking course. You have to know your audience and what its needs are. It's somebody or other's hierarchy of needs."

"Maslow," Maria piped up. "Some guy named Maslow thought this up. I had the same course."

Becky blinked. She really had given no thought to it all beyond the day-to-day necessities of life, which she was constantly struggling with. Her self-esteem? What was that?

". . . but then there is one final level – self-actualization," Jackie went on. "These are the things you do to reach your highest potential."

Becky had dumped the floor sweepings from the dust pan into the trash. Now, she lifted the trash from the can and tied a knot in the black plastic. She'd stack it at the far end of the store with the other garbage until she made her weekly run to the dump.

Highest potential was not high on her list of worldly needs at the moment.

"I'm trying to figure out what I need to do to reach my highest potential," Jackie went on. "What are the things I need to do for self-actualization?"

You are full of bullshit, Becky thought, but she kept the traitorous notion to herself. Jackie, after all, was doing a good job of filling her social needs during these lonely fall days. Becky had come to enjoy these dinnertime conversations over the cooking and the cleanup, but this time she thought Jackie was out in far left field.

Jackie rinsed the dish sponge and gave a final swirl of water to the sink. The dishes were done.

"That's why I'm taking a few months off," Jackie finished. "I'm doing a lot of meditating, thinking about what I should be doing with my life."

Oh, is that what you call it – smoking pot and staring into the flames of the fire seeking enlightenment? Again, Becky held her own counsel, not wanting to end the tenuous friendships that had come out of this time with the Phishermen vagabonds at the inn.

"How about you, Maria? What are your deepest desires?"

"Me? I just charge ahead moment to moment trying to keep my head above water."

". . . and we both ended up here."

"Yep! Go figure."

"Actually, we all three ended up here." Jackie pointed significantly at Becky.

"What? Don't mix my motivations up with yours," declared Becky.

"You're right," Jackie said. "Your motivations are different. You have Daniel to think about, and we have only ourselves, but still, we all ended up here, didn't we. We're all here, passing the time, trying to keep warm, scrambling for the next meal."

She shrugged.

"So what are the results of your meditations?" Maria interjected. "Where do you go from here?"

"I think I'll be back at Ohio State for the Spring semester. I've had enough of this lay-about."

"How do you propose to do that?"

"Hitchhike, maybe. Where's the nearest truck stop?"

Becky wasn't sure if she was grateful or appalled. Somebody, at least, had some get up and go. . . . but hitchhiking at a truck stop? Honestly!

Daniel had dozed off on the floor. Becky squatted and picked him up. He sucked his thumb and nuzzled into her shoulder. Now, how to get up? She was sure her thigh muscles could not handle the load. Daniel was getting heavier by the day.

"Here," offered Jackie.

Becky grabbed the outstretched hand and, with Jackie's help, struggled to her feet, clutching her precious bundle in the other arm. Her muscles – legs, arms, abdomen, back – all complained at the strain.

"Bedtime for Daniel."

"Yes. Goodnight, all."

Self actualization. What a concept!

Becky was quite sure she had never stumbled across it before. She had never contemplated the possibility of a highest potential.

High, higher, highest.

High, maybe. She certainly had given plenty of thought to doing a good job, to living a good life, but even higher seemed like foreign territory. She seemed to spend a lot of her time simply on maintaining the adequate.

She snuggled tightly in her quilt and listened to Daniel's slow and even breathing across the room. Tonight she lay wide awake and alone in her bed. This night certainly was filled with the adequate. She smiled at the smoldering contentment stored deep inside herself. Oh, the room itself was a bit chilly perhaps, but the pile of blankets made a warm cocoon, her stomach was full, Daniel was clean, fed, and sleeping peacefully at the end of a long day. What more could a woman ask for? What more indeed!

Self actualization! What a concept! Was she supposed to go off to the jungles of Africa with vaccinations and food boxes? Certainly there was enough need of that sort of thing right here. Was she supposed to climb Mt. Everest and brave the cold and wind and ice to reach the summit? Certainly there was enough need of that sort of thing right here. She lived it every day.

But thinking about Jackie's words, the discontentment threatened her banked fires. She recognized most of her daily pursuits as struggling to fill the very basic needs of survival and safety, with infrequent forays into fulfilling her social needs. What about that self-esteem? Was Jackie, in fact, right? Was she trying to find her self-esteem by being a good mother? Was she, in fact, trying to be a good mother because she felt a gap in her own mother's commitment? Did she become a mother because she needed to boost her self-esteem? Even, was being a good mother enough for all time, for all the nooks and crannies of her life? Her face burned as she contemplated all the nuances of this idea.

. . . and what was self-actualization anyway? Dot, dot, dash, dash. Jackie might as well have been transmitting Morse code from another planet for all that Becky understood the concept of self-actualization within the bounds of her own life.

Sleep, that most basic of needs, finally crept over her, and she nodded off, all her self-actualization puzzles unsolved.

"Becky, is there a pawn shop in town?" Lisa looked around to be sure nobody else was listening.

"A pawn shop? Whatever for?"

"I really want to go home. I really, really do."

Becky nodded. She understood thoroughly.

"What are you going to pawn?"

"My ring."

"Ahh. . . the paste one." The corners of Becky's mouth curved up, and her eyes twinkled.

"Yes." Lisa grinned.

"Where'd you get such a lovely ring?" Becky whispered so her voice would not resound throughout the inn.

"My grandmother left it to me. She died last winter." Lisa, too, kept her voice, low, confidential.

"Oh, I'm so sorry."

"So am I, actually. My parents died in an auto accident years ago, and my grandma raised me. I loved her a lot." Lisa's eyes teared up.

"It's hard to lose somebody you loved so much."

For a moment, Becky didn't know what else to say, but then a sudden alarm sounded.

"You're not going to sell it, are you?"

"No. . . . just pawn it. I can get it back later. Grandma also left me the house in Columbus. My bills are piling up unpaid while I'm gone. I was hoping the bus would finish the trip because I have no money, none, zip! I've got to get home and get a job so I can hold it all together."

"Yes, it is a real advantage having a house." Becky looked wistfully into the cavernous expanse of the kitchen, fading into cobwebs and darkness in the corners

"It's just a little two-bedroom, but it's big enough for me."

"With a two-bedroom you could take a roommate – have some money coming in."

"I do, actually – have a roommate, I mean. I texted her. She used her November rent money to pay the electric and some other bills directly, so all is not lost. . . . but I want to get back to the university for the spring semester. I was a student when Grandma was alive, but when she died everything was so confusing what with the funeral and lawyers and all that, I took some time off."

"It must have been difficult."

"Yeh! All of a sudden I had to be the adult."

"I know the feeling." Becky rolled her eyes and sighed.

"Worst of all, though, was missing Grandma. I really loved her." Lisa's eyes filled with tears. "I thought this trip to a Phish concert would be a chance to laugh again, you know, make some noise and drink some beer . . ."

"Smoke some pot . . ."

"Yeh," Lisa laughed. ". . . forget a little bit in the fun of it all, but look what it got me. Here I am -- stuck. For one thing, I'm freezing. I don't have adequate clothes. But for the other, I've been away more than two months now. I want to get home and get on with my life."

"You're not the only one."

"I'll get a job in a pizza shop or something, buy some groceries, pay the taxes. Then I can get back to classes for the spring semester."

"Sounds like a plan!"

"Do you suppose you could drive me to town to a pawn shop? When I get the money, I'll give you 20 bucks for gas. Then you can drop me off at the bus."

How could Becky deny her a trip to town with the plea put that way?

"I wouldn't let this crew see that ring, though."

"I don't. I keep it covered with this mitt most of the time."

"Good idea. They are the original Biblical plague of locusts."

"I hope you don't include me in that grouping." Lisa hugged her.

"Not at all," Becky puffed out the words from her constricted lungs, but again she wondered at her good nature. Was she just being a sucker for a good story – she'd certainly heard enough of them in the past few weeks – or was she truly doing what ought to be done to make this a better world. Where does love thy neighbor begin and where does it end?

She'd miss Lisa, though. Darn.

On the trip to town, they went by the shop that advertised "Jewelry, Gold – New and Old -- Bought and Sold." They were waited on by a sweet young woman who announced that she wanted to be a real jeweler and go to gemology school and, of course, they could mail the diamond to Columbus once the principal and interest was paid. After all, the Hope Diamond had once been delivered by the US postal service; this request for long-distance redemption was in a long and honorable tradition. Lisa got a $600 loan on the huge diamond – cash.

"Insurance when it's mailed? Yes, of course – plenty of insurance."

"Is that enough money?" inquired Becky.

"It should be. I checked the flight cost on Cliff's laptop."

Then, they drove to Wal-Mart where Lisa bought socks, sneakers, and a warm, fleece-lined, hooded sweatshirt. In the sub shop, they dined on two foot-longs – grilled chicken topped with every vegetable available except the hot peppers. Becky shared hers with Daniel, and Lisa wrapped her second half for the trip. Back in the car, Lisa donned the extra clothing, and tossed the flip-flops into her hobo bag. Lisa looked strange, unlike herself, dressed in the navy blue sweatshirt; Becky pictured Lisa always in pink with pink toenails accenting the small bare feet.

"Warmer?"

"Yes, a bit. The socks make a lot of difference actually."

Finally, Becky dropped Lisa off at the bus stop in front of the Best Western. The desk clerk confirmed their expectations. The bus was express to New York with a subway connection to JFK.

They hugged. Becky's eyes teared over.

"Hey, give me your address and phone number."

"Here's my mailing address – Grandma's house."

"Here's mine." Becky scribbled on a dog-eared notebook she found in the bottom of her purse.

"You don't have to wait."

"Yes, I do. I want to make sure you're safely on your way and not stranded again."

The bus that pulled up was polished and blue, roadworthy and solid, ready to run with the behemoths on the highway, up, up, and away, and gone.

The day was crisp and cold, and a lonely string of mare's tail clouds scudded across the clear blue sky. Becky identified with those clouds. She was going to miss Lisa, her music, her blonde-and-pink presence, her good cheer.

Neal was a prone bundle of torn hoodie, faded denim, and smelly socks emitting muffled protestations when Clifford pummeled him into handing over the keys to the bus.

"We gotta turn this baby around."

For a moment, Becky stood transfixed. Daniel was riding on her hip. Was something wrong here?

"Come on, Becky. Move your car. And spot me while I drive."

Then she realized he was talking about the bus.

"You'll never get this bus turned around in this parking lot. Ha! Ha!"

"Oh, yes, I will."

The challenge was on. The key turned in the ignition, but the bus only groaned. Clifford tried again, but the groan morphed into screeching. Finally, with a clatter and a clank, the engine caught, roaring a dark cloud of exhaust fumes out the back. Becky coughed.

"Okay. Here we go!"

The painted animals all seemed to hold their breaths and roll their eyes.

"Don't go into that ditch!" Becky waved a halt, and then motioned for him to back up. "Stop! Don't hit that porch post!"

"Couldn't they have made this road any narrower?"

"It was meant for mules."

"Hey, are you calling me a mule?"

"Well, yes, as a matter of fact."

With a deftness of a master, Clifford maneuvered the bus, 40 feet of dilapidated glory, in a 41-foot-wide space, turn after turn of the wheel as he inched its bulk around, the tires leaving geometric patterns of muddy gouges in the half-frozen edges.

Finally, the jungle-wild bus was positioned nose toward the exit – as if it were actually going to leave someday.

CHAPTER EIGHTEEN

Becky smoothed out the ticket. It was crumpled and dog-eared from days of interaction with the clutter of tissues and keys in her purse, matching the crumpled and dog-eared look of the hand that smoothed it, hands reddened from scrubbing in the cold kitchen, nails chipped from hauling wood.

Forty dollars. That was the cost of this single ticket for the Christmas Around the World house tour – six houses dressed extravagantly for the holidays, lunch at the country club, a craft boutique with items for sale – not that Becky would be able to afford anything – and all for the benefit of the women's club charities. Hmm. What she could do with an extra $40! On the other hand, she was being gifted with a day of, she could only assume, delight. At least, the lunch should be good. . . . and she never would have seen the $40 anyway. Cash was beyond Sabrina's comprehension. Presents? Yes. Presents were in; Sabrina loved to shop.

Little boys, too, were outside Sabrina's world view, and outside the experience of her friends. There, at the bottom of the printed ticket in elegant black script was the dictum: "No children, please."

"Barbara, are you working Friday? Would you be able to babysit for me?"

"I can trade for the dinner shift if you need me, Hon. I'd love to have some time with Daniel."

"What time would you have to be at work?"

"Four."

"I'll be back before then."

"Promise? Promise?"

"Yes, I promise."

"What's the matter with your housemates? Can't they sit him?"

"I don't trust a one of them. They'd be fogged out in a cloud of marijuana smoke while he climbed over the balcony railing. No thanks."

"Sure. I'll do it. He's a little love, that kid. We'll have fun. What time?"

The time on Friday was almost too early for Becky who had gotten used to mornings luxuriating in the cocoon of warmth under the quilts. The temperature usually warmed up a bit about ten or eleven after the sun had a chance to do its work, and then she got up to deal with the realities of the day. Today, however, she heeded the alarm clock. She sat up shivering, dropped her feet onto the rag rug, and hastened into her clothes. She hoped blue jeans were acceptable fashion for a holiday house tour. If not, too bad, because that was all she had.

Daniel was next. It simply was too cold for the tub; today would have to be a sponge bath. In the kitchen the teapot whistled, and she poured the water into a stainless-steel bowl, cooling it down with more water. Then, she soaked a washcloth in the water. As she washed him, Daniel complained about the cold, kicking and grabbing for his blankets. When he was clean, Becky let him keep the blanket. He clutched it to himself like the prize of a lifetime, while Becky maneuvered underneath it to tape a clean diaper in place.

"Maybe Barb can give you a full bath today. Good idea. I'll ask her."

The teapot soon had boiling water again, and she added it to two bowls of instant oatmeal. The milk was almost frozen in its plastic jug. She shook it vigorously, listening to the crystals break up, and poured a bit into each bowl.

"Come on, Big Boy. Breakfast!"

After breakfast, she started dressing Daniel – socks, jeans, tee shirt, sweater.

"Hold your foot steady," she ordered as she tried to pull Daniel's boot over a foot that moved like Jell-O inside its blue sock.

Finally, they were ready, jackets, mittens, scarves, hats, boots all in place. Becky was already exhausted. Winter is a lot of work, she mused, layers constantly coming off, layers constantly coming on. She hoped this day was going to be worth all this work. An inner excitement rumbled, though; she really wanted to have a good time. She really wanted to enjoy Sabrina's world for one day, even though she would be merely a tourist in this alien landscape.

She slung the diaper bag over one shoulder, added her purse on top of that, and picked up Daniel in the other arm. Going down the stairway, she felt top heavy, and she clutched the banister for dear life.

"Going out?"

The sleepy query came from the clutter of quilts spreading, multiplying across the dining room floor. She did not take time to identify the speaker, one wakeful person among the snorers and snufflers in the room.

"Yes."

She closed the door gently, trying not to wake them all.

Outside, flurries of snow spiraled and sparkled in between rays of sunlight. Becky looked upward to check the source of this phenomenon. Small gray clouds scurried and skated across the blue December sky, dropping their silver glitter onto the frosty landscape. The sunlight encased it all in a golden glow.

Light snow frosted the jungle bus, whirled upward in eddies, and drifted in flowing waves over the windshield, making the stranded vehicle into a loaf cake iced with meringue.

Pulling up the hill, the worn tires of her car slipped on the icy patches. "Oh, no," Becky thought. "How am I ever going to afford tires!"

The bank account barely stretched to gas. Driving into town, Becky stopped at the Exxon station and asked for $20 worth, which didn't even fill the tank. She had her route plotted out so she would not use more than two gallons today. She might even skip the Campbell mansion, which was way up on the mountain west of town. Still, she'd like to see this colonial-era stone building, one of the area's originals, all decked out for the holidays. A Colonial Christmas was promised, with bayberry, evergreens, and mulled cider to match the rag-rug-and-quilt theme of the historic house. She did like the idea of that cider; she deserved a little holiday cheer. Maybe she'd extend her budget. Guilt tickled as she handed over the twenty.

She looked to the right and then the left before pulling back on the highway, and, then, anger took over. Those damn hippies. How dare they use up her gas on their own errands! By the time she was in front of the first house searching for a parking spot, her mood had turned, and she was wishing Jackie and Maria were here with her, arm in arm, pigtails flying out from under Dollar Store knitted hats, keeping her company on this winter adventure into elegance.

This first house was the Episcopal Manse, right in the middle of the blocks of residences behind Main Street. Every curb was lined with cars, a solid phalanx of vehicles on both sides of the road as far as the eye could see. Going up the side streets, she found a parking space three blocks away. Her boots crunched on the iced-over grass as she sought the sidewalk. At least the sidewalks were sanded, ready for the ladies of the lunch set.

According to her ticket program, this elegant Victorian building done in the dark woods and embellishments of that earlier era was decorated in the English style with mistletoe balls and a Yule log.

The German style would predominate when she visited the Old Mill – with working waterwheel – that was a feature of a tourist-trap mall on the other side of town. Her parents' house, which she very well knew was a much newer, suburban developer's idea of Colonial charm, would display the contemporary American style of Christmas, while a Mediterranean-style villa, out of place on its Cape Cod-style street in Greenfield, would be turned into an Italian Christmas, with Botticelli angels. How many styles are there? Becky wondered.

The jolly old elf in his many guises from Old St. Nick through Thomas Nast's reincarnation into the modern day Santa Claus would be featured at the Country Club lobby, and lunch was being served in the dining room. Becky was already hungry for lunch.

But first, the English Christmas.

On the entry porch, she jostled with several groups of ladies lined up to enter. She definitely was underdressed. Ahead of her was a brocade jacket with a lacy black shawl covering recently coiffed hair. Beyond that a Coach purse hung, hobo style, from a wool-covered shoulder. The hats and gloves and scarves were definitely Lord and Taylor. Becky had an eye for quality – she had learned at her mother's knee, after all – and she could tell Irish wool from Taiwanese polyester. She clutched her ticket and tried not to think about it.

"Welcome, welcome, on behalf of the Woman's Club." The woman's smile was stretched so tight her teeth popped.

"Aren't you Sabrina's daughter? Why, hello. Welcome."

A warm hand came forward in greeting, and Becky felt herself being pulled into the festivities. Excited voices chattered, and the scent of evergreen permeated all.

In the living room, the fire was lit in the fireplace. Becky paused in front of it for a moment, warming her hands. She leaned down to admire the fireplace screen, a wrought iron tri-fold, with a fire-breathing dragon dominating the central panel.

At the end of the room, a small group of carolers, recruited from the Episcopal Church choir to dress in Victorian style and sing for charity, assembled. Becky joined the crowd circled around to listen.

"Christmas is coming.

The goose is getting fat.

Please put a penny in the old man's hat.

If you haven't got a penny,

A ha'-penny will do.

If you haven't got a ha'-penny,

Then, God bless you."

The crowd applauded after the traditional English Christmas song.

"Very appropriate," Becky mused as she moved into the dining room. Here, the table was set with fine bone china and glassware, as if ready for a feast. The forks rested on ironed damask napkins. Alongside the knives and spoons lay genuine English crackers, ready to be snapped and opened. Becky smiled at the thought of this family dining formally on Christmas day all wearing their king's crowns of paper.

The carolers behind her launched into "Good King Wenceslas." Their repertoire was going to be English, Becky realized. . . . and, yes, the carolers soon riffed into "Here we come a wassailing among the leaves so green."

What with a wassailing song, Becky thought there might be some cider, but, no, the drink being served in the back parlor was English tea, cream and sugar on the table, along with sugar cookies. Becky admired the silver tea service and the white linens before biting into the red sprinkles of her cookie.

Yes, there is something to this all, Becky realized. She felt quite festive, enjoying herself in the midst of this bounty as if it were her own.

She hated to leave the warmth of that first house, but then it was onward to the next. The digital sign in front of the bank on Main Street told her the temperature was 11 degrees. She shivered and tucked her blue plaid scarf – Irish wool, a prize purchase from the fall rummage sale at the church – further up her cheeks as she sought the walkway to the second house.

Finally, it was lunchtime. She pulled her battered old sedan into the Country Club parking lot, muffler shaking and singing its own stressed song of winter. She found a parking spot next to a Lexus and prayed she would not scrape it as she inched her way in.

The lobby featured a huge Christmas tree lit with white lights, gold ribbon, and gold balls, a stunning effect of absolute luxury.

Becky left her jacket and scarf at the coat check station – she supposed she'd be expected to give a tip on the way out – and went seeking Sabrina. The labyrinth of this building was familiar to her; she'd been here many times as a child eating macaroni and cheese on a Friday night while her parents dined on shrimp cocktail and steak. She soon found her mother holding court in one of the side rooms, a large table spread with white tablecloth and chairs all around. This was not going to be an intimate lunch, by any means.

"Why, Becky. How nice to see you! Where have you been hiding?"

. . . and then the question she had been dreading.

"What are you doing with yourself these days?"

"College?"

"Working?"

"No? Umm. I have a son – Daniel."

"Why, Sabrina! You have a grandson. Why didn't you tell us?"

"When was the wedding? I didn't get invited to the wedding."

Becky knew, though, that the thing to do in the face of all this was just to smile sweetly and say nothing. Let them make their own assumptions. Sabrina, too, was answering the chatter she enjoyed, and being remarkably silent over the awkward questions.

"Sabrina, your house is so marvelous."

". . . and the committee did such a good job of decorating."

"I loved those quilts on the beds. Exquisite! Are they yours? Or are they something borrowed for the event?"

"They're mine," said Sabrina triumphantly. "I made them myself."

This was the kind of small talk that made for a successful party. Sabrina glowed. Becky was glad the subject had changed away from herself.

Lunch when it came was delicious. A citrus fruit cup was the first course, and it was followed by a salad. Becky was especially glad for the salad because she had been unable to keep fresh vegetables like this ever since the Phishermen showed up, eating their way like locusts through the contents of the refrigerator. The entrée was beef tips with mushrooms and gravy over egg noodles – accompanied by seasoned mixed vegetables.

"Yum."

Becky missed eating like this. She'd be grateful when she had her kitchen back and could experiment with a few remembered favorite dishes.

She smiled broadly and chattered with the woman next to her, Elizabeth Tilyard.

"Liz. Please call me Liz," the young woman said, holding out her hand in greeting.

Becky vaguely remembered her from high school; Liz had been a senior when Becky was a bumbling freshman, wide-eyed and looking up to all those ahead of her. Liz's mother, who was seated further along the table, owned an art gallery in the Old Mill mall complex. Now, Liz was graduated from college, Becky learned, and working as a junior accountant for a company over in New Jersey. Eventually she'd be a senior corporate accountant, making twice what she was now. She forecast this with only a small hint of one-ups-manship. What else did a young woman do? Liz was a lot younger than most of the women at the table. Becky suspected she'd been invited to keep her company -- maybe be a good influence.

The chatter went on. Liz's mother was there, too, looking like an urban sophisticate in her black cowl neck knit dress, gold jewelry draped down the front. The art gallery was open today, of course, with all the people out and about, but an employee was holding down the fort.

Liz was glad she had gotten the day off from work; she had used a personal day to come to this event, she informed Becky. The house tour was so exciting, didn't you think? And the women did such a good job. The enthusiasm was breathless, and the accolades were endless.

". . . and, oh, you have a son. How nice!" Liz's pearls quivered with delight.

Becky smiled.

The dessert tray when it came was all red and green – small cakes bearing red sprinkles, gingerbread men sporting green icing overalls, sugar cookies featuring leaves and stars. Becky selected a tart from the array and focused on the sweet, melt-in-your-mouth goodness of the egg custard filling and the tang of the cherry topping. She also selected a cookie for Daniel, furtively wrapped it in a napkin, and slipped it into her purse.

When Becky got tired of the chatter of the women and the scent of Chanel No. 5, she headed to the Ladies' Room, all marble tile with potpourri bowls lined up beside the sinks. For a moment, realizing she was alone in the room, she pounded her fists on the metal walls of the toilet stall. Anger simmered underneath her breastbone. Washing her hands later, she also washed her face and rearranged her mouth into a smile suitable for the occasion.

Finally, she came back to the table, hugged her mother, waved good-bye to all the bright faces around the table, handed over a fifty-cent tip to retrieve her coat, ignored the sour look from the coat-check girl, and bundled up to leave.

. . . time to pick up Daniel.

She would miss two of the houses on the tour, but she could not keep Barb waiting. She was surfeited with good cheer for the moment, anyhow.

On the way to Barb's apartment, she took a detour past the Presbyterian Church. Here on the front lawn facing Main Street was a display that she had saved a few minutes for.

Parking was no problem here in front of the church; most of the cars in town were traveling the house-tour circuit.

She sat on the straw bale provided and contemplated the crude wooden shelter, the painted wooden oxen and sheep, the real straw heaped around the enclosure, the baby in the manger. Looking on were a loving mother, a protecting father, two awestricken shepherds, three worshipping wise men, four singing angels – and one astonished innkeeper.

Nice touch, that innkeeper, she thought, bemused.

She ought to be identifying with that loving mother, she pondered; certainly she lived that experience every day. Instead, she saw herself as the innkeeper, doling out the limited resources available and coming up short at a very important moment. He turned out to be a bad guy of this story – inadvertently perhaps, but still the one to deny this family a room.

Was Mary indignant because she had no place at the inn? She'd had to give birth in a stable. Was Joseph cross because the baby was being born on this particular night? The child could at least have waited until the next day when Joseph would have made better living arrangements. Were the shepherds fuming because they wanted to be out in the field with their new lambs? These newborns, the shepherds' worldly wealth, were at risk from night predators. Was the innkeeper furious because people kept turning up looking for a room even though he had posted a "full" sign? Maybe he wanted the means to deal with everybody's needs but simply didn't have enough resources, Becky speculated. Was he was so involved with his many responsibilities that he missed the whole point? Nobody ever talks about the anger possible in this moment in time, Becky realized; everybody focuses on the angel voices, the holy family, the love. How did they deal with the anger? The two seemed like interwoven themes to her – two sides of the same issue.

Then, she thought, nothing has changed from there to here.

Before she left, she said a prayer. Dear God, keep me in love. Please protect us. – and, oh, yeh – help me deal with this never-ending rage. Amen.

CHAPTER NINETEEN

The river stretched like a lion too long asleep on its veldt of frozen ground, rumbled in the night with a primordial groaning. Becky, awake and in awe at the river's wintertime song of the ice, shivered underneath her quilt.

Freezing on the river starts with ice crystals forming on weeds, and then stretches out a translucent film in the sheltered pockets between rocks. Like a lake, a river freezes from the shoreline out, but, unlike a lake, which freezes gently, seemingly overnight, into a glassy surface, drawing delight from would-be skaters and ice sailors, the river with its moving water fights the freeze, contorting and splintering, heaving over huge chunks of ice, tossing them shoreward like the playthings of a wayward giant. The whipped white solid, churning into a mass of mud-dredged blocks and angles, piles higher, tearing chunks of shoreline and tumbling boulders into the constantly changing patterns of the riverbank. Through it all, the river keeps rolling downhill, its great mass of water questing for the sea through unfrozen mid-river channel or splintered fissure, billions of gallons draining a watershed awash with winter's frenzy.

December at the Duck Point Inn was a challenge. As the temperature plummeted, Becky wheedled the Phishermen into the bar room with the wood stove. Forget the marijuana updraft; she had found that she could close off this room and keep it and her bedroom above reasonably warm. The room soon took on the appearance of a hamster cage.

The tables and chairs formed a rickety structure of upside-down and nestled seats, backs, and legs shoved to one end. The floor space disappeared under mattresses and quilts as the Phishermen abandoned beds in distant, freezing corners of the inn in favor of the shared body heat that added to the comfort on these cold days and nights. With this room so crowded, Becky began living almost completely in the bedroom upstairs. She moved her television and microwave upstairs where these appliances had to share the single outlet with the floor lamp and the hot pot.

Every day began with filling the wood stove. Sometimes the coals were still smoldering underneath a blanket of white ash. Sometimes the coals were out but the firebox was still hot. Whichever, somebody soon had the fire started and the warmth radiating into the room. The Phishermen, in a day-long frenzy, had chopped and stacked three cords of wood, and Becky praised God for the foresight of this burst of energy.

"Warming us twice," Cliff commented.

"A Robert Frost poem?"

"Duh! I don't know. I'm a business major." Neal quivered his upper lip at the sentiment.

After the fire was stoked, Becky would check the bottled water, stashed a few feet from the stove, to see if it had frozen overnight. Most mornings Neal could make coffee. The coffee mugs were the only dishes the group dirtied all day, and everybody was responsible for cleaning, by whatever means possible, his own cup.

By evening, they had the room almost cozy and could play cards or listen to Susan play the guitar. They all got used to trekking to the outhouse when necessary, and hand wipes served for hand washing and face washing.

Twice a week, Becky put on her boots and parka, dressed Daniel until he looked like a cocoon, got in her sedan, and crawled up the lane, sanding over spots where snow or run off had iced it over, emerging triumphantly, again, out of the evergreen-forested tunnel of the lane onto the highway and into town. Sometimes these outings were grocery or garbage runs. Other times she trekked to the swimming pool at Greenfield High School. She spent a lot of time in the shower in the locker room with Daniel, using the bountiful hot water, getting clean, getting warm. She and Daniel would come home smelling like chlorine and shampoo. She was afraid they'd smell the pool on her and insist on joining the swimming experience.

Most of the Phishermen didn't bother at all with washing, and the smell of the crowded bar room was getting rank.

Cope, Becky reminded herself.

"We could find you an apartment. Nobody expects you to endure the coldest winter on record down here." Parker was getting really concerned about her well-being. ". . . or why don't tyou go stay with your parents?"

"I haven't got the money for the security deposit, and my parents haven't asked me to move back. Can't I come stay with you?" She smiled her sweetest, most reassuring smile. Even Parker did not know about her growing stash of money; she hadn't told anybody. It wasn't just the issue of the security deposit, though. She did not have enough income for rent on her own. Surely he knew that by now. But his log cabin was toasty warm and completely adequate.

"I cannot have you come stay with me."

Disappointment, so heavy it sank in waves like frigid air to the floor, swept over Becky.

"I'm sorry, Hon. I really am. I don't own that cabin. I share it with another ranger –it's like a bunk house, really – and my Park Service supervisor says 'no' to live-in girlfriends." Parker shrugged a shoulder forward in commiseration and pecked on her cheek.

Becky pursed her mouth and stared at the knot-holed ceiling beams, wondering just who was saying no.

Becky grimaced at still another icicle nose. Daniel was sitting up in his crib, though, ready for another day, and she knew somebody must get up to feed the stove. She hoped it would be one of the sleepers below. Warmth. Would it ever return?

She looked out the window at the river and was astonished at the view. Ice. The river was iced almost all the way across, with blocks and chunks sticking skyward. In the middle, a narrow channel allowed the river to flow.

"Does it ever freeze all the way across?" Becky had asked Parker.

"No. At least it had better not."

"Why do you say that?"

The water has to have somewhere to go. If it froze completely, we'd get a flood."

"Aha."

As Christmas approached, Parker spent more and more time at the inn.

"Winter is a quiet season for me," he explained. "During the summer, I hardly get to breathe, what with all the tourists and all the activity. But in the winter, I can take some time off."

For the first snow, he brought three sleds, huge, fluorescent ovals of plastic for riding down the hill. They tucked Daniel into his jacket and snow pants and ran out to enjoy the white wilderness, slogging in their boots through the drifts, throwing snowballs at each other, laughing. Afterward, the inn was a surprisingly warm haven.

Parker had brought takeout Chinese, a treat just for the three of them, and they went to her room to hide out and enjoy it. First, there was the tang of hot and sour soup, then the oily goodness of egg rolls, and finally the filling heat of Szechuan chicken and broccoli. Becky licked her lips when she was done; she licked her fingers. Then, Parker was licking her fingers. She felt the heat rise throughout her body and knew that it was not the food causing this surge in temperature. His hand went under her sweater, exploring, caressing.

"Oh, God. I'd better take Daniel downstairs. They'll babysit for a while."

"Yes, you do that." He grinned.

She came back upstairs to find that he had turned down the quilt and was sitting on the edge of the bed, boots off, parka thrown aside, waiting for her. She quivered at the sight.

He grinned at her and beckoned her to join him. She went to him eagerly, kicking off her sneakers on the way to the bed. He pulled her to him in a long kiss and then pulled the covers over the two of them, exploring shapes and forms as the bed warmed up. Laughing, they kept the quilts over them as they pulled off sweaters and jeans, mashing socks into the crevices, entwining legs and torsos, enjoying the touch of body heat in the chill. He kissed her cheeks, her forehead, her nose. She smiled into the pocket of warmth they shared and let her tongue linger on his chest.

Cleaving unto him, finding in him an amazingly competent lover, Becky breathlessly, bountifully, recklessly fell head over heels into a passion she had never known before. Parker enjoyed every minute of her falling.

"I'm glad you're enjoying this," he whispered in her ear, brushing it with his tongue for good measure.

"Ah, yes," she replied with abandon, and she arched her body, asking for more.

Becky-and-Parker-in-love was the catalyst for the Christmas spirit that began to spread throughout the inn. Neal smirked at her over morning coffee, but she ignored his knowing glances. Neal, in turn, ignored her aren't-you-going-home-for-Christmas comments. Amid much laughing, the whole group erected a Christmas tree cut from the woods. They went into the Yule with cranberry and popcorn strings tangled up with kisses. The twosomes seemed fresher, more loving, happier to be with each other, funnier. Through it all, celebrating the coming of God's child of love, Becky and Parker clung to each other in the full heat of passion and the first flush of love.

CHAPTER TWENTY

Through it all, the river kept on freezing.

Parker, keeping track officially, mounted an outdoor thermometer, and Becky got used to seeing the black pointer bypassing the painted red cardinal on the upper dial, seeking out the stark-black, five-below mark in the first light of morning.

"It's really cold early this year," he commented pulling on his olive-green parka, huddling inside the brown faux fur trim on the hood.

They had plenty of time to talk on these lazy days off. They never ran out of interesting things to chatter about.

During one of their conversations, he explained to her the intricacies of his job. The National Park Service has different kinds of rangers, he told her. Some people are hired as local rangers. They have expertise of one kind or another that pertains to a specific locality, and they are hired to use their skills or knowledge for that particular place. They will probably stay in that one place their entire time of service, and can set up a home and a life, expecting to stay.

Others, though, are hired at an administrative level. These rangers move around a lot, spending a year or two or three at one park and then moving to another, as the Park Service needs them. Parker was one of these latter types of rangers. He expected to work all around the country before he was through. Some rangers might eventually get to a level that would take them to Washington to work in offices there, and then they'd settle down, maybe in the Maryland suburbs, but Parker didn't want that. He wanted to be out in the field, working with the rivers, the woods, the trees, and the animals – and with the people who visited to see and enjoy these rivers, woods, trees and animals.

"I might spend a winter in Yellowstone," he told her. "I'd have a cabin somewhere, and I'd have to stock up the pantry before the snow fell because there wouldn't be any travel in or out of the park."

". . . but why hole up like that?" Becky could not quite picture the scene.

"Somebody has to keep an eye on the park over the winter, to know what's going on."

"What would you do to amuse yourself?"

"Oh, there's plenty to do – snowmobiling is great, and the animals are fun to watch."

"But aren't the animals in hibernation?"

"Not all of them."

"Brrr. Sounds cold to me."

Parker laughed, and added, teasing her.

". . . but my next assignment might be at St. John in the Virgin Islands. I'm sure you would not get cold there."

"Oh, am I going to be there with you?" Her mouth turned up in a wicked grin, and she looked at him appraisingly.

"You bet." He, too, grinned. "What an interesting upbringing that would be for Daniel."

She chalked it up to snuggling talk, chatter under the covers, but still she wondered – Was he really thinking that way? . . . and how did she feel about it all? A cabin in Yellowstone? Hmm. Feeding a wood stove? Well, that was exactly what she was doing now.

Parker used his cell phone to check in periodically from his holiday, which was spent mostly in Becky's bed. Becky and Parker snuggled under the quilts. The cell phone lay on the bedside stand, and, when the signal wavered, periodic trips up to the main road connected them to another world where responsibility waited. She began to understand that was the way it always would be in their relationship because that was the way it always would be in Parker's life. Leaning on her elbow, scanning his face as he talked, she came to know that she liked it that way.

The vacation was interrupted, though, when Parker's cell phone on the bedside table suddenly rang shrilly in the pre-dawn hours.

Startled, Becky opened her eyes to see the gray mound that was Parker already sitting up, reaching for the phone with one hand and his khaki-green pants with the other.

The unexpected signal cut off though; the call was detoured to voice mail. Parker checked the list of missed calls.

"Gotta go, Hon." He kissed her and pulled on his parka. "It's work. I'd better go find out what they want."

Then, with the bang of a shutting door, the muffled thuds of his boots on the stairs, the far-away turning over of the truck engine, the crunch of snow tires on the ice and snow of the driveway, he was gone.

Later, when she turned on the television, there it was on the morning news. Ice blocks were catching in the trees on Makepeace Island. An ice jam was forming. Becky looked at the female newscaster, obviously freezing despite a black wool coat and red hat and mittens. She was silhouetted against the dirty white of river ice. "Coldest year on record." She was quoting the weather service and . . .

Why, there is Parker!

Being interviewed.

How nice!

Becky grinned at the flickering images and blew a kiss of pride in the direction of the television. Whatever it was that had to be handled, she knew Parker could handle it.

"Jingle bells, jingle bells, jingle all the way."

Becky grimaced and forced her face into a smile. Her father, the banker who could not sing, was getting into the spirit of the season and trying to entertain his grandson. He was down on all fours on the floor being the horse for the holiday sleigh. Becky had never thought she would see the day.

"Here, Dear. Have some more coffee."

Christmas morning brunch at her parents' house was a mixed blessing. They had feasted on eggs and bacon, and lingered over the home-made streusel coffee cake. Becky hugged the coffee cup to her bosom, grateful for the warmth, even in a warm house. It was getting harder and harder to shake the bone-chilling freeze of the inn.

Certainly she was grateful for the matching stacks of presents that had been handed to her and Daniel. She was happy with the jeans and the sweatshirts, the socks, and even the new electric blanket that came her way, but she was embarrassed by the bounty given to her. Her offerings, a Wal-Mart sweater for each of her parents – as if they did not have enough sweaters stacked upstairs in the drawers, as if they did not have central heating that poured out the 21st century warmth – did not seem like much in comparison.

Her discomfort did not last for long, though, because there was a compelling topic to talk about.

"What about the ice, Parker? I hear the river is freezing hard this year. People are talking about a winter-time flood." Becky's father's face had the appropriate somberness for such a serious subject.

Becky felt the twang, twang, twang of inappropriateness. To her, this was not a conversation for a brunch table with white tablecloth and holly centerpiece. Her father should come down to the inn and see the river in action, grinding logs and chicken coops, and wooden steps along in its wake, see the great blender of freeze at its vicious worst, see how cold they all were living there beside the river. Then he would know some of the truth about the reality of life instead of sitting here on the other side of the holiday candles, buttering a crescent roll and making conversation. She gritted her teeth.

Parker carried his end of the conversation with a smile, though. "Yes, we're having a hard freeze this year."

"We require flood insurance for any mortgage for a building on the flood plain," Becky saw the firmness on her father's face as he arrived at his favorite topic, banking. ". . . slows down the building in these low-lying spots, that's for sure."

Becky drummed her fingers on the table, bored.

"Not every lender requires this, though," he went on. "Some buildings down there have no flood insurance."

Parker nodded. He actually looked interested. ". . . could be a real disaster, especially a wintertime flood when this weather will make it even more dangerous. The zero temperatures will hinder the cleanup, too."

Becky took some bacon, crumpling half for Daniel, who had been stuffing scrambled eggs into his mouth, spoon and fingers having equal success at getting the food where it was meant to go.

"People are going to be homeless if it happens," Parker added.

"Yes, and I'm glad we live up here in the hills a bit. The water won't come up this high."

You mean more people homeless than just me? Becky looked up, suddenly interested in the conversation. In a flash, she understood the tangled interrelationships – her mother, the housewife on Baker's Farm Road, taking pristine care of her treasure; her father, the banker, worrying about everybody's treasure; and herself, the homeless, not yet come to an understanding of how to gain the treasure, how to deal with the human cost of a house, the financial cost! Why, she wanted the same thing out of life that they did! She was astonished at this revelation. Understanding opened up like a curtain opening in her brain.

"We are working on that ice jam. Want to come with me and see what all the shouting is about?"

"Sure." Anywhere that Parker wanted to go, Becky was willing to follow.

The pickup truck was coming off the mountain now, into town.

"There, look!"

She heard the river before she saw it, a guttural roar of water confined beyond the capacity of mere ice blocks to confine it. She saw the white, slushy river rising almost to the level of the trusses of the Greenfield bridge. Water, dark and sinister, curled onto the low banks, threatening waterfront houses. The river seemed twice as wide as normal and a thousand times more powerful, with a medieval dragon writhing underneath the tangled ice, heaving and groaning to be set free. Becky was in awe.

Further south, the parking lot at the overlook by Makepeace Island was full – cars, vans, even a fire truck pasted a colorful human mosaic against the primordial panorama of the ice. Parker moved an orange cone and pulled into the spot he had saved for himself.

"Did you ever see Hell freeze over? Well, here it is." He beckoned for her to come and look.

First, with the automatic action of a mother, Becky checked Daniel. He was asleep in his car seat in the back of the truck. She grinned at his ease, head to one side in a gentle snore. Then, joining Parker, she walked over to the cemented stone wall at the edge of the overlook.

She saw the river, a slushy mass rising up through the dark trees. Where was the water? There was no dark channel here, no constant flow — just this ice mass, blocks tumbled over blocks, rising higher and higher, the river's power turning upward as the only direction to go.

Becky could see the ice jam a quarter mile downriver. A mountain of white blocks tangled among the jackstraws of the trees of Makepeace Island, and thrust itself skyward. There was no engineering in this dam, just the pure chaos of nature which was reasserting its dominance over the creatures that stood beside the ice looking on. The water could not move past this phenomenon of winter, and instead was rising.

Becky understood the danger in one instant. "Phew!"

"Hey, Becky." One of the coveralled, fur-hatted figures waved to her. Now she could see it was Dave, their barbecue pal, who walked toward her, carrying a gas-powered chain saw. It was nice to be recognized here. She knew it was because of Parker, but still she liked the feeling of welcome. She had been too isolated for too long.

"What are you guys doing here?" Becky inquired.

"We've been trying to cut up some of the blocks with chain saws, hoping something would break loose and start moving," Dave reported. ". . . but it's really dangerous to be out on the ice doing that."

"Dynamite!"

"What did you say?"

"Dynamite. That's what you need."

Dave threw back his head and laughed. "Quite a girlfriend you've got here, Parker," he said putting the chain saw into the back of his pickup.

Becky writhed in embarrassment. "Well, I watch enough TV."

Parker chuckled. "Actually, we have called for a demolitions team. That's the next step."

Dynamite! Hmm.

That's what it would take, too, to break up the ice jam of comatose people, huddled under quilts at the inn, passing around still another joint. A good blast of dynamite, placed just so behind that bus, and they would be jet-propelled back to Columbus.

Becky laughed to herself at the cartoon image forming in her mind of a quilt-cushioned package being blasted west on Route 80 all the way to the Ohio border, uphill, downhill, a vanishing streak of dirty, flying-carpet-like quilts, just like the Roadrunner of Saturday morning cartoon fame. Beep! Beep! Gone!

She chuckled out loud then. She would light the fuse.

CHAPTER TWENTY-ONE

"**W**ho the hell are all you people?"

In the kitchen, Becky heard the commotion, a stentorian voice blasting a halt to the hum of the inn, even though she didn't hear all the words. She went bursting through the swinging doors to see what was going on.

"What the hell are you doing here?"

The man was tall, white-haired, and tanned. Becky thought he would start frothing at the mouth any minute, he was so rabid with anger. The twosomes sat at attention amid their mounds of multi-colored quilts, wide-eyed, staring at the apparition.

"Lou sent us." The minute the words were out of her mouth Becky realized how absurd they sounded.

"Lou? That son-of-a-bitch! Well, Lou doesn't own this place. I do, and his lease is up — ended November thirtieth, and good riddance. I came up from Florida to reclaim my property, and I find it full of a bunch of hippies, druggies, no-good lay-abouts. I want you all out of here right now! Out! Out!"

"Twenty-four hours," Neal Hamilton negotiated. "We'll clean up after ourselves."

For once, Becky blessed Neal's quick thinking, his uncanny ability to manipulate people. Everybody else was still sitting or standing with their jaws down around their belly buttons, and Neal had come up with a retort that might buy them some time.

"What did you say?"

"Twenty-four hours. We have to make some arrangements. We have no bus driver, and these people can't just walk out of here." Neal waved his hands across the room, a sea of casts and white bandages. "Give us 24 hours, and we'll clean the place up before we go."

The man looked quizzically at the recovery ward in front of him.

"What happened to all of you people, anyhow?"

"Bus accident."

"How'd you get here?"

"Lou sent us."

"Ah, Lou, that son-of-a-bitch. I bet he did this to me on purpose." He raised his arms heavenward as if invoking the gods. Then, he turned to Neal Hamilton.

"Well, Lou's lease is up – and I want you all out. Twenty-four hours, not a minute more. After that, if there's anybody left, I'll call the State Police and have you all arrested as trespassers. Understand?"

"Yes, sir – and a Merry Christmas to you, too."

The man turned and stalked out the doorway, descended the wide board steps, crunched across the driveway, revved up a Dodge Ram van, and spun snow, gravel, and leaf mulch as he sped from the parking lot to the lane.

"Wait! Wait!"

Becky raced after him, but she was too late. She had been stunned by this apparition, but, a split second too late, it occurred to her that she was not evacuating to Columbus, Ohio, with the rest of the group. She had nowhere to go.

She turned and looked at the ramshackle inn where she had been so improbably happy.

Homeless again!

"Call Lou."

"Sure thing."

She grabbed Neal's cell phone, opened it, pushed the start/end button, and got some momentary flashing lights followed by a notice that the battery was low and this cell phone was powering down. Some interesting, powering-down music accompanied the rolling flashes of red that died away to black.

"Damn!"

"Does anybody have a cell phone that works?"

What a stupid question. With an intermittent, almost non-existent signal, nobody had bothered recharging. The faces looked back at them pale and uncomprehending in the cold, morning light.

"Well, plug it in." Neal's voice was full of disdain, and she counted to ten as she inserted the metal prong into the side of the phone.

They couldn't wait, though. A working phone was needed ASAP. Becky drove – as usual – to the diner. Neal was surprisingly silent.

Becky found Barb flipping two slices of toast onto the cutting board.

"I don't suppose you've seen Lou!"

"Nope. I heard he went to Florida for the winter."

The butter ran yellow, melting into the hot toast, Becky pictured Lou melting like that butter onto a beach of toasted yellow sand. He'd never come back, and she'd never get out of this fix.

Then, she borrowed Barb's phone, dialed, and listened to a computer-generated voice tell her that Lou's number was no longer in service.

She gritted her teeth. "He probably knew all hell was going to break loose."

"He probably planned it that way," Neal said. "Letting us create havoc to get back at this guy."

Becky's eyes opened wide. She could not conceive of some-body making a plan like this – play 20 unsuspecting people to irritate one – but it all made sense – a conniving, calculating scheme.

Neal went on, "You probably were the plan. We just dropped into his lap – fortuitously. Lou manipulated us all to get back at that guy, whoever he is."

Becky stared at Neal. It takes a manipulator to know a manipu-lator, she thought. Yes, it surely does.

Becky braked the sedan in front of the county jail and gave a sudden turn to the wheel. She heard the blaring of horns behind her as she entered the jail parking lot. A sudden determination infused her back-bone. The key to this conundrum was here, incarcerated behind bars. With a driver, this busload of misfits could be on its way, heading west.

"Good idea," pitched in Neal from the seat beside her,

"You go in and get him out. No, better – we both will go in."

She parked the car, and, with determination, got out. Neal slinked behind her. At the entrance to the jail, she pushed the bell and heard a faraway buzz.

A disembodied voice came through the speaker. "Yes?"

"We want to talk to . . ."

"What's his name?" she whispered to Neal.

"Harry Milton," he whispered back. Then, he spoke into the speaker. "Harry Milton. We want to visit Harry Milton."

Becky heard the click of the automatic locks, and the door slid open.

"Come in," invited the disembodied voice.

They stepped through the doorway into the shadowed hallway. The door shut and locked automatically behind them. Becky heard the click of the locks in the door in front. The second door slid open. They stepped into the gloom. Becky felt uneasy as the second door slid in place and clicked to a lock behind her. In front of them was barred window opening onto a barred cubicle where a uniformed guard was stationed. She cleared her throat and found her voice.

"Harry Milton, please."

"Sign in that book and show me your picture ID."

The sign-in book had six columns – date, name, address, relationship, etc., etc. Writing through frustration, the process seemed impassable to Becky.

"How do we get Harry Milton out of here?"

"He has a $10,000 bail."

"Erp."

"I could have told you that," piped up Neal.

"You could do it with cash or a property bond, or a bondsman will cost you 10 percent. You make arrangements at the office at the courthouse."

No matter about financial arrangements; this bail was beyond comprehension.

"I want to talk to him."

"Are you on his list of visitors?" The official voice droned out the unexpected question.

"I am," interjected Neal. "Let us visit with him."

They were ushered to a concrete block room painted in a color that may once have been yellow. An expressionless guard motioned for them to stand, and he used a scanner on both of them to make sure that neither one had a gun or a knife or any other dangerous contraband on their person.

After an interminable wait, apparently to ascertain if Harry wanted to add Becky to his list of approved visitors, Neal and Becky were ushered into the interview room. Here was more concrete block, this time painted a putrid green. No comforts existed here, she noticed. She settled down on the hard plastic stool provided in the visitation cubicle, and Neal stood behind.

"So, Harry," demanded Becky to the pallid, orange-clad man on the other side of the glass and wire mesh. "What are we going to do about getting these people back to Columbus?"

She tried to look like an avenging angel, come to Earth to demand retribution from Harry. She knew she was not pulling it off.

"What do you want me to do about it?"

"This is not my problem," she declared through clenched teeth. "It is your problem."

His eyes opened wide in surprise. The concept of a responsibility here seemed to be a new one.

"I suppose you've got my bus."

"Yes, we're taking good care of the bus for you."

He licked his lips.

"Maybe my brother."

"What about your brother?"

"He has a commercial license. This is his bus, too. Maybe he can fly out and drive it back."

"Good idea. Why didn't somebody think of this before? How do we get in touch with your brother?"

Becky was near tears as they returned to the car. She brushed them away with a fleece-gloved hand and waited for her eyes to adjust to the sunlight.

Then, it was back to the diner. The sun was sinking into the west, and a chilly wind whistled at Becky's back as she tucked her hands into her pockets and headed across the parking lot. Barb didn't say a word, just reached for the phone, rolling her eyes as she handed it over.

Fortunately – amazingly – the brother was home. For sure, something had gone right – for once – in this farce.

Becky carefully explained the situation. She tried to sound official, with that courteously demanding edge to the voice that Parker affected when he was on duty.

"Why sure," the brother replied. "Send me the airfare, and I'll be happy to fly out."

"No airfare," she sputtered. "This is your responsibility. You will pay the airfare and chalk it up as a business expense."

"I don't have the money to fly out there, nor do I have the money to fill the tank to bring that bus back to Columbus. Harry has the company credit card."

She took a deep breath.

"I think," she intoned ponderously, "that if you do not do something here – and right away – that there will be suits – law suits. We have some very angry people here. This is your responsibility."

Of course, she knew she was the main one who was angry; the others concerned were just lying around, stoned out of their minds, waiting for some miracle to happen – or maybe not happen. She wasn't sure they even grasped the reality of the situation, but she certainly wanted them out of her hair. She listened with satisfaction to the sudden, contemplative silence on the other end of the line.

"Okay," he said reluctantly. "I will fly into Newark Airport. Can somebody pick me up?"

"Sure." She felt she could be magnanimous here. But then she jumped in with, "As long as you are prepared to pay for the parking fee and gas."

"What?" he fumbled.

"Law suits! Remember the law suits!"

Becky gave a thumbs up to Neal, and then dialed Parker. She was grateful to hear his voice, grateful to hand a little bit of this predicament off to his hands. He would deal with it, she knew.

She described the events of the morning.

"That was Nate," Parker told her.

"Nate?"

"Yeh. Big man? Big shoulders? White hair?"

"Yes."

"I guess he owns the place. Lou is a renter. They're friends really, but, hey, money is money. Say? Is Nate kicking you out, too?"

"Sure sounded like that to me."

"You know, if he gives an eviction notice, I might be assigned to come along with the sheriff to serve it."

"What? Parker, are you serious? Would you actually evict me?" Becky's hackles rose. She had lowered her guard for Parker, trusted him. She had forgotten he was, in effect, a policeman.

"No, I don't think I could do that. I'd claim conflict of interest. I suppose I could pass it off to the State Police."

But it was already too late. The fingers of anxiety were running up and down her spine, the drum laces were tightening upon her stomach.

As Becky returned to the car, she became aware of Neal, waiting in the car for her to finish the business at hand. She saw him wink at her through the layer of glass. She watched this as if from a distance, dispassionately, but she was not exactly clueless at what transpired next.

He turned sideways in the seat, acting nonchalant.

"Why don't you come with us?"

"Nah. I can't do that."

"Sure you could. What have you got holding you here?"

She decided to get right to the point. "Are you propositioning me, Neal Hamilton?"

"Sure." He grinned, an ear-to-ear affectation that left Becky cold. "I've got an apartment two blocks from Ohio State – and a double bed."

The roulette wheel in Becky's head was spinning, momentarily gone berserk. Going with Neal Hamilton would certainly solve her sudden housing emergency. Being in such a propitious environment might even enable her to get some education, which, God knew, she needed. In another lifetime she might have said yes. But the wheel turning in her head clicked down to a sudden halt on no.

"No. Absolutely not. Never."

"Okay. Just asking."

He didn't even care! Becky twisted her face in disgust. Well, good riddance to this crew.

She threw the car in gear with a fury born of disappointment. Parker, too! He could just go to hell.

The hot tears fell.

CHAPTER TWENTY-TWO

The ice storm began during the night. Waking in the muted dawn, Becky heard the snap, crackle, pop on the porch roof and looked outside.

Aiee, she thought. Ice was the main thing she was afraid of at the inn. Already she had learned its power over the switchback gravel lane. A good ice storm could strand them all down here at the bottom of an impassable climb.

Over in the corner, the recharged cell phone rang, and she went rummaging for it among the library books and old magazines on the corner table.

For once there was a signal. It was Parker, terse and to the point. "I think you should leave now."

"Bad ice storm?" The adrenalin started pumping.

"Yes, but that is just adding to the problem. We have a solid ice jam here at Makepeace Island. The dynamite hasn't budged it. I'm down here now with some experts trying to figure out what to do. The water is backing up behind it, and major flooding is expected. Greenfield is at risk, and Greenfield bridge is being threatened by the ice. Who knows what's going to happen up there at the inn. It's a very dangerous situation brewing."

When she looked out the window, her eyes flew open. Even in the dim light of this late dawn, she could see that the water had risen onto the bank overnight.

"We'll be on our way," she told Parker.

She got dressed in a flash. Adrenalin could do amazing things to the human body, she realized.

"Okay. Everybody up. We're outta here."

Becky addressed the inert mound of quilts on the floor of the dining room.

"Oh, come on, Becky. Have a heart," wailed a plaintive voice from underneath the mound.

"Water's rising. A flood is expected. We gotta get outta here."

She lifted quilts amid muttering and dire threats until she found Neal. She shook him by the shoulder.

"This is no foolin'. We're in danger here."

Neal sat up blinking the sleep from his eyes.

"What the hell? It's not even light yet."

"Flood! The river's flooding."

Understanding flickered across his face, and he bounded into action.

"Everybody up!"

Good! He was taking charge of the horde, pulling off quilts, shaking sleepers. Bed heads began to emerge with hair sticking up every which way; dirty sweatshirts followed. The entire mound was alive now and writhing with people turning, stretching, groping, yawning.

Becky turned and went back up the stairs. Daniel was still in his crib. Becky pulled fresh clothes out of his drawer, changed and dressed him. Her mind raced with anxiety. She pulled on his jacket and boots, cap down over his forehead. She threw on her own parka and boots, checked that gloves were in her pocket, found the car keys in her purse, and, slinging diaper bag and purse onto her shoulder, hoisted Daniel into her arms to go downstairs.

The Phishermen were ready to go, too. They had been sleeping in their clothes for weeks now, so getting dressed was an unnecessary step. Lacking warm coats, they had thrown the multi-purpose quilts around themselves whenever they had gone to the outhouse. This they had done now, so that the group looked like a walking, moving version of the sleeping mound that a few minutes before had been on the floor. The body smell wafted through the room.

Becky waited until they all had exited and then locked the door behind herself. Navigating the porch under the roof was no problem. At the porch steps, though, she paused. Ice glazed everything – steps, railing, walkway, parking lot, car, forest beyond. The world was a marzipan fantasy, a glass spectacular like those for sale in the mall at Christmas time.

Ahead of her, the mound of quilts quivered and shivered, a red and blue and green living creature, changing shape with each step or slip, arms flailing occasionally to keep the balance.

Becky stood Daniel on the porch and tested the steps. Her foot slipped, and she skateboarded off, crashing down all three steps to the ground. She gasped for breath. Her back hurt ; she'd be black and blue tomorrow. This is not a good idea, she reflected. Lucky I didn't break something. Gritting her teeth against the pain, she grabbed the railing and pulled herself upright. The world is an ice-skating rink, she realized. How fast that had happened! Lifting Daniel to the ground, she made him walk – or, rather, slide to the car. The ice was not to his liking. He scooted along on his bottom, getting his jeans wet as he went.

The moving mound of quilts was in trouble. She could see ups and downs and hesitations that meant they were slipping and sliding, too. Every once in a while she could see a crutch emerge from the mass, adding whiskers of wood to the amoeba. She wondered how Susan and Mary Ellen were managing with their casts.

Daniel wailed in the car seat, an unhappy, wet, cold little boy while she scraped the windshield. She could see two dark figures, arms reaching upward, working on the bus windshield. They were going to have trouble finishing that job, she could see. The car crunched through the ice to the gravel of the parking lot, but the ice on the lane was already beyond hope. She drove 10 feet, got out, and salted the lane. She drove another 10 feet, got out, and salted the lane. She had a quarter of a mile to go. I am not going to have enough salt, she realized. The Phishermen were still working on their windshield. Daniel screamed in her ear as she punched the numbers on the cell phone.

The signal was there, thank God.

"Parker, I can't get up the hill."

"You have to get up the hill, Hon. The river is rising fast; you're in danger there."

"But this old inn has been here for a couple hundred years or so. Nothing has flooded it yet." Becky was cold and wet and tired, and the thought of the inn, with its wood stove and warmth, sounded really appealing. She could almost call it home now. She grimaced, biting the inside of her check in her agony of indecision.

She heard the gurgle and crack of ice shifting on the river. Looking in that direction through the silvery haze of falling sleet, she could see a fullness to the river that had not been there before. It was rising. Parker was not fooling her. Water was curling around ice chunks, lifting them and moving them. From this distance it looked like a vanilla Slushee spill, and the Slushee flow was moving in the direction of the inn. Now, dark liquid lapped at the dark wood of the river-side deck, and the rickety steps canted downstream. Another nail or two, and they would be on their way into the jumble of broken tree limbs, rank vegetation, churned ice, and frigid water that was grinding its way downriver.

The car would not move. She had used her entire supply of salt, and she was only a hundred yards up the hill. They could sit here in the car – she supposed they were above any potential flood level now – but the gas would only last just so long, and, when that ran out, they would be out of heat.

Besides -- there were those Phishermen. Two dark figures were still working on the bus windshield. The rest of the moving mass had poured itself into the bus doorway, and the people were now sitting on the cold, hard-plastic-cushioned seats, waiting for the bus to move.

"Get that hunk of junk out the way," Neal shouted. "The bus is heavier. Maybe it can negotiate the ice."

The back windshield was still a solid sheet of ice. Becky backed down the lane, head turned watching her way through the open driver-side door. With the car down on the flat parking lot again and out of the way, she motioned for Neal to try it with the bus.

He nodded and threw the bus in gear. At the first turn, the rear of the bus slid in slow motion off the road and crunched downward into the rhododendron leaving a smear of black oil through the ice coating into the leaf mold and rot of the forest floor.

Becky could hear the screaming through the glazed blue windows, shaking the crystalized silence of the glazed blue world.

"Stop! Stop! Everybody quiet," Neal was commanding them as Becky struggled upward toward the bus.

"Stay away," he commanded as she approached. "I'm going to try to get out of here."

He threw the bus in gear, and, with a mighty roar, it lurched upward a few feet – and, then settled downward even deeper into the shrubbery.

Could Parker come and get them? The four-wheel-drive pickup truck should be able to navigate the ice on this driveway. That's what four-wheel drives were for. Dare she ring him up and ask him? Becky scrunched her face in dismay. She had already learned the downside of a relationship with a law-enforcement official. He was busy. He was rescuing a town. Besides, he was 45 minutes away at Makepeace Island, trying to deal with the emergency there. Becky took a deep breath and knew that this little rescue – of Daniel and herself and the Phishermen, all of them, quilts and crutches and casts and all – was up to her. She felt the grit rise up her backbone, stiffening it for action.

Now, just how was she going to pull this off?

Then, she remembered the crampons.

They were still hanging there in the inn's store on the wall, waiting hopefully for somebody, anybody to buy them. She could use those crampons to walk out of here! There were enough crampons for a dozen people to walk up that hill.

But what about Daniel? She knew she could never negotiate the ice, even with crampons, off balance carrying a heavy load like Daniel.

. . . and what about the people on crutches, with casts.

Then, she remembered the sleds.

Her face lit up! She could do it; she knew she could.

She threw the car in reverse and backed down the incline, across the parking lot, sliding sideways into her accustomed spot.

"Sit tight, Daniel."

He didn't have any choice, belted into his car seat the way he was, but he bellowed again as she left him.

Carefully negotiating the ice, she let herself into the inn, in her purposefulness ignoring its warmth. Opening the door to the store she made her way down the counter. There they were, hanging like a row of monster teeth from their leather straps. She went back though the warmth, grabbing a blanket and cookies and juice on the way through the building, and exited the front door again. The sleds were on the porch. With the blanket, she made a nest on a sled for Daniel with a flap to pull over the top of him. Then, she put on the unfamiliar crampons, and began to walk to the car.

They worked. Becky smiled her satisfaction as she heard the muffled crunch of steel points denting the ice. Coming across the parking lot, her walk had a satisfying steadiness that had not been there before. She pulled the sleds behind her, fanned out at the ends of their ropes.

Daniel was screaming, a full-blown tantrum in progress in the back seat of the car.

"Please, Daniel," she said. "We don't have time for this."

She wiped his nose and then handed him an apple-juice box, straw at the ready. When he had settled down and drunk a little, she handed him the cookie. Then, she struggled with the straps holding his car seat firmly in the back seat of the car.

She was getting cold and eager for action to warm her up.

Finally, she lifted the car seat out of the car and onto the sled.

"Sleigh ride, Daniel." She forced her voice into a playtime lilt.

With the euphemistic prospect of a fun time ahead, Daniel settled down into the car seat that she strapped onto the sled. She pulled the blanket flap over him to protect him from the incessant sleet. She took the rope handle to his sled in one hand and the ropes to the two larger sleds in the other.

She enjoyed this new-found confidence. This was the feeling she had been seeking when she decided to raise Daniel on her own. This was the feeling that had been hiding behind chairs, skulking underneath couches, skittering around corners for the past two years, instead of settling on her shoulders where it belonged. Yes! She could do it by herself.

Then, in a last minute concession to practicality, she called Parker on the cell phone.

"We're walking out. Do you suppose somebody could meet us at the highway?"

"Wait, wait, wait!"

"No wait. The river is rising – it really is – and I am not getting drowned or frozen standing here. Just send somebody to meet us at the highway sign."

She set off across the parking lot. Yes! This was working. Foot by slow foot she progressed, pulling the sled behind her. The incline was more difficult, but the crampons bit in and she kept climbing.

At the bus, the group was milling around, semi-interested faces emerging from the shrouded multi-colored mass. She handed the rest of the crampons to the men and passed over the ropes of the two sleds.

"We're going to have to walk out." Her voice had taken on a definitive edge. She heard it crackling back at her in the echo of the ice.

"How are these people on crutches going to walk out?" Neal's voice was testy.

"They go on the sleds. The others pull."

"Not me. I am not pulling. Not in this ice." Neal's voice was as cold as the lash of the ice on Becky's face.

Becky felt the last set of crampons being ripped out of her hands. Neal had claimed them.

"What are you doing?"

". . . getting ready to hike up that hill. What does it look like I'm doing?"

"People with crampons will have to help those who don't have them."

"Who says? I've done enough for this crazy crew. I'm not helping." He knelt to buckle the crampons onto his worn Timberland boots.

Becky's mouth fell open in astonishment. "Well, I'll be damned."

"It's okay, Becky," said Clifford, his voice soft and patient. "There are enough of us to help. We'll make it."

Clifford's quilt stretched out tent-like to encompass the sled. Becky could see Mary Ellen emerge from the depths of the bus, folding herself into a sitting position on the sled. Somebody handed her a pair of crutches that she laid diagonally across her lap. Somebody else tucked a quilt over her head and shoulders, protecting her from the sleet. Becky could see that a similar maneuver was under way with Susan. A few people without crampons had grouped with people with crampons; they'd support each other. Turning to start up the hill, she could see Neal, a ghostly figure making its way through the sleet ahead of them.

"This is not going to be easy." Clifford's voice sounded muffled in her ear.

"No, but we can do it."

For a moment, though, she was disoriented. The broad, dark bulk of the bus was no longer by her side giving stability to the universe. Her world became a white swirl of snow and ice. Beyond this circle of sight was the unfathomable blackness of a December morning, the shortest days of the year. She was suddenly spinning in this whiteout. Which way was up? Which way was down? She paused to consider gravity. Her feet were down, so her head must be up, but – which way was the road?

A hand reached out of the swirling chaos and tugged on her arm.

"This way, Becky." Clifford's voice was muffled. "This way."

She put one foot after another and found that the land did, in fact, rise before her. Her feet were climbing; she recognized the muscle pattern of climbing, even if she couldn't see the road. Now, if she just did not fall into the rhododendron.

She saw a black bulk just behind her – Clifford pulling his sled. The cell phone rang in her pocket. Of course, it was Parker.

"Are you okay? Where are you?"

"Parker, I'm scared."

"Where are you?" His voice had an edge of panic.

"We're coming up the driveway. There's a group of us together. Just be waiting."

Climbing the hill, she felt energized by the exercise, feeling a sweat forming in her armpits. The rope bit into her gloves, numbing her fingers. Keep going. She knew it was important to just keep going, to keep putting one foot in front of the other, to conquer this hill, to not stop, to not let the ice take over. Step by step she put the crampons into the ice. Step by step she climbed. She could sense the others coming, too, hearing the crunching as crampons bit ice, sensing an occasional curse, seeing the ghostly shadows in front and behind her as they all struggled up from the wilderness.

There! She was up the hill and into the straight stretch. Evergreen boughs loaded with ice slalomed on either side of her. The little orange plastic sled bobbed along behind her like a cork in a sea of ice. The Duck Point Inn sign was just ahead. She could see the faded, red-speckled belly of that ridiculous fish. Good, because she was getting really cold now. A row of vehicles waited, headlights and searchlights throwing strong beams into the reflecting storm, hot exhaust rising in luminescent clouds around the dark, welcoming corps of vehicles. She saw the ambulances and a big passenger van. Was that Parker himself just ahead with the four-wheel-drive pickup truck, jumping up and down with excitement? Yes. Then, he bundled her into the warmth – he had kept the heater going, bless his heart. He lifted Daniel out of his blanket nest, and put him into the back seat of the truck. Blessed warmth. She peeled off her gloves, ice to the core, and laid them on the floor, holding her hands to the steam of air from the heater. Then, she cried.

"Do you need an ambulance?"

Parker was all compassion as he echoed her long-ago words of greeting to him. She could feel the edge of his concern in his voice.

"No. I'm all right, really. Check Daniel."

"He's fine. He was as cozy as a bug in a rug in that sled."

"He got wet sliding on the ice."

"We'll have him safe inside the truck in a jiffy."

"Thanks for coming for me. I guess you do rescue damsels in distress."

"Yes, that's my job, Hon." He laughed.

"I'm glad I'm on your list." She grinned.

"Of course you are. You're my treasure. That's why I came myself."

"How are the others?"

"Cold. Frostbitten. They were not dressed very adequately. We are taking the whole bunch to the hospital to be checked out."

"I don't have to worry about them anymore?"

"Nope. I am officially pulling the plug on that, Hon. They are all going to the emergency room, and from there they can make their own arrangements, wherever they want to go. It's not your worry anymore."

She laid her head back against the seat, breathing the warmth with every grateful pore, feeling the guilt with every thawing nerve.

She should have gotten them out sooner. She should have kept track of the weather reports better. She'd like to be saying goody-bye to Jackie and Maria, at least.

"I guess I have trouble disconnecting from responsibilities, even when they are not my own."

He laughed and threw the truck into gear.

"Girl after my own heart."

Then, he added, "You got everybody out of there. Did a damn good job. I'm proud of you."

He was proud of her? It was a new sensation to have somebody be proud of her. She felt her frosty facial muscles turn upward as a grin became the center of a brand-new universe.

Becky waited in the pickup truck, heat on high, for Parker to finish being official and take her somewhere for the night. She longed to go to Parker's cabin with its brick-red and ivory quilt, but she knew that was not a permanent option. Where could she go? Her parents' house? Oh, yes, that was the only answer.

"We'll get your stuff out in a few days, Hon – as soon as this ice lets up," Parker promised in the midst of the bus frenzy.

In the meantime, not only was she homeless again, but her car, her clothing, her quilts, her groceries – everything but she and Daniel, the car seat, and the clothes on their backs – were stuck down in the Duck Point Inn, at the bottom of that chasm of ice.

She had never been so totally devoid of resources since that first weekend when she had left her parents' home, eager to start a life on her own for herself and her coming child.

This time, though, she did not feel adrift on a sea of want. The difference, she knew, was sitting in the driver's seat beside her – Parker, smiling at her, glad of her presence. She leaned over against him, smelling wet wool and sweat, and feeling the heat of his cheek and breath.

"Where to, Hon?"

She sighed as she settled back into the passenger seat. "Let's head south. I need a warm beach after all this."

His eyebrows arched over his aviator sunglasses, a tangle of joyful surprise, as if he was deliriously happy at the possibility. He ginned ear to ear.

"Guess what? The word just came through; I'm being transferred to St. John in the fall. Wanna go with me?"

Suddenly the double arch of her eyebrows mirrored his; she stared at him. He was giving her a future with him. Taking a deep breath, she found her voice. "Of course!" Then, thinking her soft rasp would be interpreted as a lack of enthusiasm, she pulled herself together with a loud "Yes! Yes!"

She felt like one of those high-school-band marchers, beating on the big bass drum of her heart, calling the cadence for a life of joy with Parker.

"I should warn you though – I do not want an only-child family. I'm hoping for three or four more to keep Daniel company. Are you up to that?"

"Well, maybe one or two more. Let's not get carried away with this. Remember we'll be living in the backside of nowhere most of the time."

His laugh boomed throughout the pickup truck. Becky thought she could happily listen to that laugh for the rest of her life.

CHAPTER TWENTY-THREE

Becky awoke the next morning inside a glow of pink blossoms.

For a moment, she was confused. Sleep came and went. Her eyes were baffled by the brightness.

Then, she focused and recognized the contours of the room. She was back in her childhood bedroom, staring around herself at Sabrina's trellised fantasy. Sunlight blazed in the window, overpowering the sheer white curtains and boiling over into the far corners. The room was marvelously warm.

Daniel? Where was Daniel?

She lifted herself onto one elbow, and scanned the lower half of the room. There, beyond the maple footboard rose the plastic rim of a portable crib. She threw off the blankets and clambered onto her knees to peek over. Daniel was lying on his side, sound asleep, covers in disarray. One bare leg splayed outward. His thumb was in his mouth.

We have to do something about that thumb, she thought.

Was that the only thing she had to complain about this morning? Then it all came flooding back to her – she was alive. Daniel was alive. They both were safe – and warm, too, as it turned out. What more could she ask for?

She turned to that overly bright window and looked outside. The whole world glistened with ice. Every tree branch, every blade of grass, every surface, was covered and mirroring sunlight. Branches snapped and crackled. What a difference from the day before! This morning was a lacy wonderland backlit by a triumphant sun moving upward in the bright blue bowl of sky.

She moved to the edge of the bed and looked for her sneakers. No sneakers! She remembered she'd hiked out in snow boots. Her sneakers were still at the inn. How about her clothes? Umm, umm! She was wearing an unfamiliar oversized tee shirt. Oh, my!

She wrapped a sheet around herself and pattered downstairs in her bare feet. The floor was cold, and she shivered.

Her father was in the kitchen, humming loudly to himself.

"Well, there you are. The coffee's made. Do you want some breakfast?"

"What's for breakfast?

"Pancakes and eggs."

"Of course – your specialty. Sounds great, but let me get some coffee first."

"Your clothes are in the dryer. Your mother washed everything."

"Oh, thanks."

Becky poured herself a cup of coffee and added sugar and milk. She sipped the top half inch of liquid, enjoying the rich Colombian aroma and taste. Then, she hiked the sheet up in one hand with the coffee cup in the other and moved to the breakfast table.

"Where'd you get the portable crib?"

"I borrowed it from the Osborne's. They keep it for when grandchildren come to visit."

"I suspect we're here for more than a visit."

"That's okay. We'll make it work." He sat down across from Becky and smiled tentatively.

". . . if that's okay with you, I mean." Becky colored, realizing she had invited herself to stay. She put her palm up to her forehead. She had been taught manners, she remembered – right here in this very house.

One of those never-ending aphorisms sprang into her mind.

"Guests and fish spoil after three days."

"Well, you're neither guests nor fish, so I do not expect you to turn rotten on me."

Becky smiled.

"Where's Mom?"

"Down at the firehouse making sandwiches."

"Sandwiches?"

"Yes, the firemen are all out dealing with the ice jam on the river and the flood. The Auxiliary is feeding them."

Becky tilted her head. She was perplexed.

"I didn't know she was in the fire auxiliary."

"Yes, her friend Jane Meyers convinced her that the fire auxiliary would be a good deed. You know – Lady Bountiful and all that   the lady of the manor."

"Oh, I see."

"She thinks we don't understand her, but we do, don't we?" He winked.

"She went out in this ice! Amazing!"

"She has four-wheel drive in her SUV."

For a moment, they sat companionably, drinking their coffee. Then, Andrew spoke up.

"Becky, I've been wrong, we've all been wrong, in allowing this rift to come between us. I'm glad you're home. I hope you'll stay for a while."

"A while!" She affirmed it carefully. "I will work at it; I really will."

"So will I."

Daniel sounded a fire-siren wail from the bedroom upstairs. He'd woken up in a strange place and realized his mother was not there with him. Becky jumped up.

"Oh, get the clothes from the dryer."

She retrieved them, hanging onto the sheet with one arm, and headed up the stairs. A few minutes later she came back down, dressed in her own jeans and sweat shirt, Daniel cleaned up, diapered, and dressed, to find pancakes in production.

There was no high chair, so Becky sat Daniel on her lap to eat.

"I'm so glad we're getting this chance to talk," Andrew said. We need to do this – to talk about the past and the future, and how we feel about things."

"Dad, looking ahead to the future, I really want to get together with Parker. He's a good man. We work well together, and we have a lot of fun together. What's more, I trust him with my life. There's no BS there."

"Love him?"

"Yes. Of course."

"Then, go for it."

He flipped a pancake in the pan, turning a golden side up.

"I am. I definitely am – going for it, I mean. We don't have anything definite planned, yet; please understand that. I may be here for a while. We're looking ahead to fall."

"What are you going to do in the meantime? I mean, you're welcome to live here, don't get me wrong, but with your mother and all that, it would be better if you had some kind of an activity during the daytime so you're not underfoot all the time."

Becky sighed.

"I'm not throwing you out." He sat up in an alert pose. His voice was anxious. "Please! I'm just talking about keeping the pressure off her. How many pancakes do you want?"

"I understand. We all have to accommodate ourselves to make this work. Two – two pancakes, and Daniel will eat one."

She thought for a moment. "Actually, I think I'd like to go to the community college."

"Oh, really." He smiled broadly. ". . . taking business, perhaps? Going into banking? A chip off the old block? You can take over from me as vice president when I retire." His mood was jovial at the possibility.

"I dunno." She shrugged. "I'd like to do some exploring of what's available. You know, start with the basics and see how it goes from there."

"I don't think I'll be able to pay tuition. The credit card really is stretched to the max." For a moment, he hunched over the frying pan avoiding her eye.

Oh, honestly, the voice sounded in Becky's head. . . . that same old subject. Give it a rest!

"I'll try to get financial aid, Dad. I've been living on my own; I know how hard it is to make ends meet."

His body relaxed. He handed her a plateful of pancakes and eggs easy-over. Then, he hugged her.

"I'm sorry the budget is so strung out; your mom lives our lifestyle to the max. You know how she is. I'm really glad you've got plans, and I'm glad you've gotten away from that bunch of losers."

She cringed and shook her head. "Losers? Not all of them. They were not all alike. I'm going to miss some of them. You know, Dad, if there is one thing I have learned this fall, it is that people come in many different varieties."

"They sure do. Syrup?"

". . . and they certainly do not fit into simple categories. People who seem alike because of one characteristic may be entirely different in another. We can't put them into little groupings and think they're all alike. They're not."

He nodded sagely.

"I mean, this is not a one-size-fits-all world, and we have to accommodate ourselves to the idea that not everybody is alike. It's not all about me and doing things the way I might like. Neither is it all about somebody else and doing things the way they might like. We have to compromise with each other so we can live in harmony, so everybody can live happily and grow into the very best person they can possibly be."

". . . a very important concept in life." His balding head increased its front and back momentum as he affirmed her words. One white strand fell loose onto his forehead, standing out starkly against the tanned and freckled expanse.

"Everybody has a right to be happy."

He handed her a fork.

". . . self-actualization, and all that. . ." Her voice trailed off. "I am going to miss some of those people."

She stopped talking long enough to fill her mouth with pancakes and syrup. Daniel fussed over missing his sippy cup.

"Here. Drink from this glass." He grasped the unfamiliar glass and drank. Enough milk went into his mouth to satisfy him. Becky retrieved the glass and used a napkin to wipe away the dribble on his chin.

The crunch of icy gravel on the driveway alerted them to the SUV coming into the driveway.

"Mom's home."

Becky struggled with Daniel on her lap, while Andrew collected empty plates. The back door opened with a rush of frigid air and a stamping of boots on the entry mat.

"Oh, look, you're all awake." Sabrina was all smiles; her morning out had done her good. She gave hugs and kisses all around.

"I see you found your clothes."

"Yes."

"Becky, dear. Those jeans are ragged at the cuffs – and that sweat shirt is faded beyond belief. We've got to get you some better clothes than this. What will people think?"

Some things, Becky realized – some things will never change.

CHAPTER TWENTY-FOUR

The bus was not as lucky as the people. Little by little, it slid down the glazed incline, sunset view first, until the rear wheels were resting on the ice at river's edge. Then, in a groan of axles and ice, the bus moved onto the frozen mass where it sat in regal splendor, a multi-colored magnificence, an ark of jungle lushness, amid the dirty white ice blocks grinding their way down the river.

The Greenfield Fire Department was frantic. The National Park Service was anxious. Ecologists were concerned on behalf of the heron and the shad. Businessmen were livid on behalf of the tourists, who, with money in their pockets to spend, come looking in season for the heron and the shad.

Somehow they had to get this bus off the ice before it deposited its load of oil and axle grease and gasoline into the pristine environment of the river. All possibility of dynamiting the ice jam was on hold because of the fear of sinking that bus.

Ice climbers, with crampons and helmets, made their way down to the bus with the thought of attaching a cable. Pennsylvania did not boast a cable long enough to reach the bus at the bottom of the Duck Point Inn gorge, so the firemen patched together many cables, linked like a paper-clip chain, and tried to attach a hook to the bus. They missed. The floe moved away from the shore, and the climbers leapt to safety just in time.

Parker took Becky to an overlook to see the bus moving down the river afloat on a floe, escaped from the reality of earth like an ark adrift on a prehistoric flood.

Her mouth opened in amazement.

"Actually, it'll be easier to catch a little further down the river where the banks aren't so steep." Parker tied to sound hopeful, but he bushed his hair back in a gesture of desperation.

CNN came to cover the story, and their vans and crews clogged up the local roads for days. Town residents got used to the sight of Maxwell Carter, front-lit by portable lights, disks and tripods, camera men with heavy cameras on their shoulders, discussing the fate of the bus, of the Delaware River, and of the Duck Point Inn. Becky, dressed in the new jeans and new sweatshirt, with new boots, new knitted cap and mittens, new plaid scarf, got used to being interviewed. She was the only remaining survivor of the rescue; everybody else had suddenly found the resources and high-tailed it back to Columbus, Ohio, as fast as they could go – except, of course, for Harry Milton who still was a guest at the county jail.

"God speed," Becky wished the Phishermen, blowing kisses and thankfulness westward.

The bus floated in magnificence under the Greenfield Bridge, giving a view of the painted roof, ocelots and iguanas, macaws and monkeys, two by two, in all their jungle wildness just beneath the ice-coated trusses. All traffic came to a halt to watch. Police cars blocked both ends of the bridge, cruiser lights rotating a red-and-blue warning, preventing automobile access. Firemen dangled from the bridge, assessing the situation. Christmas lights, still in place, cast a multi-colored glow across their stalwart faces.

"Great shot," declared Maxwell Carter to everybody present and nobody in particular.

Parker looked grim. He threw the pickup truck into gear and headed down the river road, the vanguard of a string of emergency vehicles heading for the overlook at Makepeace Island. A horde of people was in place watching as the ice floe bearing the bus ground to a halt on the ice jam at Makepeace Island, vibrating the ice and the earth itself. Water rose up behind the floe and washed across the face of it, the river clutching its prey in a final engulfing embrace. In a flash, emergency personnel were on the floe, had chains secured to the front and back bumpers of the bus, and began the winching that eventually would bring the errant vehicle back to the road, where it sat for all the world like a jungle creature captured, dazed by the photographers' flashbulbs, waiting for native bearers to hoist it shoulder high and begin the trek into captivity.

Finally, a fireman dared to approach. He got in the bus, turned the key, which Neal had inadvertently left in the ignition, and drove it back to town, accompanied by the entire parade of police cruisers with sirens blaring and firemen's vehicles with flashing blue lights piercing the dimness of the December afternoon. The high school band, which had been assembling to play at a New Year's Eve dinner/ dance at the firehouse – wondering if there were going to be any firemen at the dance, since they were all out chasing down a jungle-wild bus – met the parade and piped it into town with a fanfare of trumpets and drums. Holiday lights blazed a greeting.

Behind the parade, a fountain of ice and slush and muddy water rocketed skyward as the demolitions experts finally ignited the dynamite that opened a channel in the ice jam. With a greedy sucking at rocks and ice blocks, spraying white in its eagerness to roll, the water found its opening and the river became a river again.

Somebody, who knows who in the darkness of a December night, set off some New Year's Eve fireworks, and the red and green starbursts exploded high in the darkened sky.

The firemen went home to shower and change for the party. Their wives cheered.

Neal got a ticket for polluting the river – plus a ticket for driving the bus without a commercial license. He waved to them jauntily as he boarded the Greyhound bus for New York.

The January thaw opened up the dirt road down to the Duck Point Inn, and Parker, after contacting Nate for permission, drove Becky in the truck one Sunday to collect her belongings. She was astonished at the stark appearance of the inn; the silhouette of the building stood out like a black scarecrow against the radiant white of the surrounding landscape. How had she ever thought this place was welcoming?

"It's amazing this place didn't float away with the bus."

"Yes, those old-timers who built this place knew what they were doing. It's just high enough to escape the floods."

She still had the key; she turned it in the lock and entered. The building was eerily silent. The dining room was freezing, even worse than the outdoors temperature. The ashes of that last fire lay gray and damp in the firebox of the stone fireplace. A clutter of grimy quilts lay across the bare wood floor; the tables and chairs were pushed back and piled up against the wall, one on top of the other. She wondered if she should clean up that mess, too.

She remembered Tim's backpack and wondered if he had gotten that magic sack out of here. She tried to picture him as they all made the trek out – Did he have it on his back? – but the events of that night were so muddled in her mind that she could not remember.

Out of habit, she flicked a light switch, but nothing happened. Then, she remembered; the electricity was turned off.

Upstairs, Parker took apart the crib. She packed her clothes into black garbage bags and was taking one downstairs to load into the back of the pickup when she heard a familiar throaty roar. This roar came down the entrance road, snaking into the parking lot, getting closer and closer, louder and louder. The world was suddenly full of the sound of bikes, many bikes, bikes of every description -- black bikes, red bikes, green bikes, with black leather jackets, black boots, blue faceplates, silver faceplates, helmets with flames and helmets with zig-zags, helmets with alien faces, mustaches curled and flaring to the sides, women riding behind and clinging to the drivers, pony tails flopping from behind the helmets – all descending through the scrim of leafless trees down the gravel and slush into the parking lot.

For a moment, Becky stood stunned.

They kept coming. She faced a parking lot full of bikers and their big, black, mighty bikes, overpowering the whole scene with their noise.

Her mouth fell open. She blinked her eyes to be sure she was awake. She dropped the bag and moved forward off the step and into the parking area. Finding her voice, she asked, "Can I help you?"

The biker on the lead motorcycle turned off his ignition and dismounted. He hit the kickstand and turned toward Becky, removing his helmet as he ambled over. She saw a neon-red and cobalt-blue Mohawk rising from an otherwise bald head.

Please, God. No! Not more people seeking a room for the night.

"Closed! Closed! Closed!"

"We are closed." She wasn't sure they could hear her over the noise of many motors still roaring their road rage behind him.

What was the sign language for "closed"? She drew a blank on that one, but she rose up on her toes and threw her arms back and forth in what she hoped was an approximation of "no."

Then, she took a firm footing and squared her shoulders in determination. Without her willing it, without her even thinking the gesture through, her right hand rose into the firm, upright, palm-front position that means "stop."

"No room at the inn," she yelled over the roar that filled the parking lot. She was sure that they would not hear her authoritarian voice with its unwelcoming, rancid Yule-tide joke, but she hoped they'd understand the negative connotation of her voice and hand.

The dismounted biker turned to the others and gave a shushing motion with his finger. The level of sound diminished as the bikers ceased their revving. For a moment, it was unnaturally quiet. The lead biker walked up to her – he was a bit too close, as a matter of fact; she took a step backwards – and then he shouted.

"I am so sorry," he said. "We made a wrong turn."

She looked at him quizzically.

"You're not staying?"

"No. We're on a rally – Izzy's Icicle Run." He paused and apparently decided she needed a bit more explanation. ". . . two hundred bikers going fifty miles through the back roads of Pennsylvania and New York state with an Italian feast at the end – our way to celebrate the New Year."

"Aha!" Her face showed partial enlightenment. She understood the rally and feast part, but two hundred motorcycles in this parking lot? She shook her head in bewilderment at that.

"Our map showed a right turn. We turned at that sign up there, but apparently that was not the right right turn." He smiled at his own little joke.

"Are you going upriver or down?"

"Up through Pennsylvania and then down through New York state. We make a circle. Then, we get to eat, drink, and dance. Later on, we'll get to . . . Well, you know! " He winked.

"Go back up to the main road. A bridge across to New York state is about 15 or so miles north. That's probably your turn."

"We do apologize for disturbing you. We'll be on our way."

He stepped back and gave a courtly bow, holding the black helmet to attention under his left arm and swishing his black-gauntleted right hand through the air to accent his graceful movement. It was a perfect imitation of Sir Lancelot greeting his queen. The Mohawk even worked well with the gesture; for a brief moment Becky pictured the brush fringe on the top of a knight's helmet. The images from the many books she had devoured flashed through her head.

Becky curtsied in reply and smiled an impish grin at the biker.

"Be careful on that driveway; it's really icy."

"We will."

Then, she had a sudden thought. "What road are you circling south on later?"

He gestured with his leather-gloved hand beyond the inn to the cliff on the other side of the icy river expanse. "We'll be coming down that road right across there, the one on the cliff face."

She laughed out loud. "I'll hear you."

"Oh?"

"Yeh. I'll stick around until you guys go past. This is something I want to experience."

She waved a farewell as the lead biker remounted, kicked his stand up again, and started his ignition. He took the lead, and all two hundred bikes fell into line, circling around with a military precision that left Becky breathless. She could envision the legions of Rome finessing a marching maneuver.

Parker wouldn't understand the delay, Becky thought – but then again, he might; he seemed to appreciate the bizarre. As she turned, she saw that he had come out behind her. He had been watching the whole thing,

"Boy, Hon," he said sardonically. "You've really got that no-room-at-the-inn routine down pat."

"Parker," she said. "Parker, we've got to stay awhile. Warm up the truck so we can wait. You've got to hear this – two hundred motor-cycles roaring past that cliff face. Wow!"

The End